Stay with me.

Sarah wasn't sure she'd heard Aiden's words correctly. They were surprising. They were scary—driving her to a place where she surrendered to her deep longing for him.

He granted the smallest fragment of a smile, looking at her with his heartbreaking blue eyes. He tenderly tucked her hair behind her ear, drawing his finger along her jaw to her chin. "I don't know what force in the universe brought you to me, Sarah. I only know that right now I need you. I want you. And I'd like to think that you want me, too."

The air stood still, but Sarah swayed, light-headed from Aiden's words. Their one night together had been electric, filling her head with memories she'd never surrender, but judging by the deep timbre of Aiden's voice, they might shatter what happened in Miami. "I don't want to ruin our friendship." *And no strings attached only breaks my heart.*

"Is that why you shut things down after Miami?"

"Yes." It wasn't the whole truth, but it was enough. As much as sleeping with Aiden might be a mistake, she didn't want to deprive herself of him. Would one more time really hurt? "And I've spent the last two nights regretting it."

"Then I say we have no more regrets."

Before she knew what was happening, he scooped her up into his arms.

* * *

Ten-Day Baby Takeover is part of Harlequin Desire's #1 bestselling series, Billionaires and Babies: Powerful men...wrapped around their babies' little fingers.

Dear Reader,

Thank you for picking up *The Ten-Day Baby Takeover*! It's the third book centered on the Langford siblings, and I have loved chronicling their dysfunctional dynamic. This story starts five months after *Pregnant by the Rival CEO* and is about Aiden, the mysterious older brother who has come home to New York to make peace with his family. Little does he know he's about to get a family of his own!

As an author, some books come together easily and some are an endless source of frustration. I wouldn't say that *The Ten-Day Baby Takeover* came "easily," but Aiden certainly materialized before my eyes like magic. I've been thinking about him for two books, so I guess my brain was ready to put him center stage.

Writing Aiden's story was so satisfying. He's everything I love in a hero—strong, the lone wolf, the one who claims he's not capable of being hurt, or capable of loving anyone. I won't spoil the story, but the arrival of the son he didn't know he had and his temporary caregiver, outspoken Sarah, brings big parts of Aiden's past to the surface. Deeply painful Langford family secrets come out—things we've wanted to know about for three books! In the end, only loving Sarah and sweet baby Oliver can make his heart whole again. I really hope you enjoy it!

Last, for anyone wanting to know whether Anna Langford and her husband, Jacob, had a girl or a boy, you'll find that out, too!

Please drop me a line any time at karen@karenbooth.net. I love hearing from readers!

Karen

KAREN BOOTH

—

THE TEN-DAY BABY TAKEOVER

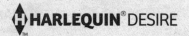

Recycling programs
for this product may
not exist in your area.

ISBN-13: 978-0-373-83836-3

The Ten-Day Baby Takeover

Copyright © 2017 by Karen Booth

Printed in U.S.A.

Karen Booth is a Midwestern girl transplanted in the South, raised on '80s music, Judy Blume and the films of John Hughes. She writes sexy big-city love stories. When she takes a break from the art of romance, she's teaching her kids about good music, honing her Southern cooking skills or sweet-talking her husband into whipping up a batch of cocktails. Find out more about Karen at karenbooth.net.

Books by Karen Booth

Harlequin Desire

That Night with the CEO
Pregnant by the Rival CEO
The CEO Daddy Next Door
The Best Man's Baby
The Ten-Day Baby Takeover

Visit her Author Profile page at Harlequin.com, or karenbooth.net, for more titles.

For my dear friend in the writing world and the real world, Margaret Ethridge. I will always want to stay up way past my bedtime, talking and giggling in the dark with you.

One

The lobby of LangTel's Manhattan headquarters was practically a shrine to order and quiet restraint. It was not the place to bring a fussy baby. Sarah Daltrey had done precisely that. Marble floors, towering ceilings and huge expanses of windows facing the street made any sound, especially baby Oliver's errant cries, echo and reverberate like crazy.

Sarah kissed his forehead, bouncing him on her hip as she paced in the postage stamp waiting area. For such a massive building, taking up nearly an entire city block, LangTel had been distinctly stingy with the amenities for the uninvited. Two chairs and a ten-by-ten rug sat opposite a closely guarded bank of elevators. It was clear that no one occupying this space should stay for long.

Oliver whimpered and buried his head in her neck. Poor little guy—none of this was his fault. Oliver hadn't asked to take a four-hour train ride that morning. He certainly hadn't asked to come to an ice-cold office building in the middle of his nap time. More than anything, Oliver hadn't asked to lose his mother three weeks ago, nor had he asked to have a father who refused to acknowledge his existence.

Sarah took her cell phone and dialed the number she'd memorized but wasn't about to add to her contacts. As soon as she got Oliver's dad to accept his paternal responsibility, she'd force herself to forget the string of digits that led to an office somewhere in this building, most likely the top floor. There would be no maintaining ties with Aiden Langford. Their connection was temporary, albeit of paramount importance. She had his son and he was going to take custody, even if it killed her.

"Yes. Hello. It's Sarah Daltrey. I'm calling for Aiden Langford. Again."

One of the two security guards manning the lobby gave her the side-eye. Meanwhile, the woman on the other end of the phone line expressed equal disdain with her snippy tone. "Mr. Langford has told me a dozen times. He does not know you. Please stop calling."

"I can't stop calling until he finally talks to me."

"Perhaps I can help you."

"No. You can't. This is a personal matter and Mr. Langford should appreciate that I'm not sharing the details of this situation with his assistant. I outlined it all in the email I sent to him." *More like seven emails, but who's counting?* "If I can just have five minutes of his time, I can explain everything." Five minutes was a lie. She'd need at least an hour to walk Mr. Langford through Oliver's schedule, his likes and dislikes, and to make sure he was off to as good a start as possible.

"Mr. Langford is very busy. I can't put through the call of every person who claims to need his time."

"Look. I just spent four hours on a train from Boston to New York and I'm downstairs in the lobby, caring for a ten-month-old sorely in need of a nap. I'm not leaving until I speak to him. I'll sleep here if I have to."

"I can have security escort you from the building, Ms. Daltrey. Surely you don't want that."

"Does LangTel want the embarrassment of their security removing a kicking and screaming woman with a baby from their lobby?"

Mr. Langford's assistant said everything with her momentary silence. "Can you hold, please? I'll see if there's anything I can do."

Sarah had very little hope for this, but what other options did she have? "Sure. I'll hold."

Just then, a statuesque woman with glossy brown hair dressed in a tailored gray dress and black pumps came through the revolving door. Sarah might not have noticed her, but she had a baby bump that was impossible to miss. The security guard beelined to her, taking the stack of papers in her arms. "Good afternoon, Ms. Langford. I'll get the elevator."

Anna Langford. Sarah recognized her now, from the research she'd done on the Langford family while trying to find a way to get to Aiden. Anna was one of two

LangTel CEOs, along with her brother Adam. She was also Aiden Langford's younger sister.

Oliver dropped his favorite toy, a stuffed turtle, and unleashed a piercing wail. Sarah cringed, crouching down, scooting across the carpet in her wedge sandals, scrambling for Oliver's toy while cradling the phone between her ear and shoulder. Anna came to a dead stop and turned her head, zeroing in on Sarah and Oliver.

Great. Now we really are going to get kicked out of the lobby.

Anna frowned and strode closer, but when she removed her sunglasses, there was only empathy in her eyes. "Oh no. Somebody's unhappy."

Certain that she'd been banished to the land of horrible hold music, Sarah ended her call and tucked her phone into the diaper bag. "Sorry about that. It's nap time. He's tired." When she straightened to face Anna, she felt as if she needed a step stool. Anna was tall *and* in heels, while Sarah was height challenged even in her strappy sandals.

Anna shook her head. "Please don't apologize. This is the highlight of my day. He's adorable." She reached for Oliver's pudgy hand and smiled. He responded by gripping her finger, his head resting on Sarah's shoulder. "I'm Anna Langford, by the way."

"I'm Sarah. Daltrey. This is Oliver." Sarah watched as Oliver smiled shyly at Anna. He was such a sweet and trusting boy. Saying goodbye to him was going to be heartbreaking, especially after three weeks of caring for him all on her own, but that was her charge and there was nothing to be done about that. She was done with being a nanny, and caring for a child that wasn't her own, regardless of the circumstances, felt far too much like her old life.

Anna's eyes didn't stray from Oliver. "Nice to meet you both. I'm due to have my own little one in about six weeks. Middle of June. I have baby fever right now, big time." She studied the baby's face. "Your son's eyes are incredible. Such a brilliant shade of blue."

And exactly like your brother's.

Sarah cleared her throat. "He's not mine, technically. I'm his legal guardian. I'm in the process of connecting him with his father. That's why I'm here."

Confusion crossed Anna's face. "At LangTel. The father works here?"

Sarah had committed herself to discretion for the sake of everyone, especially Oliver, but this might be her one real chance to get to Aiden. She was getting nowhere with his assistant. "I came to see Aiden Langford. He's your brother, right? I need to speak to him about Oliver, but he won't take my phone calls."

"Oh." A flicker of surprise crossed Anna's face as her eyes darted between Oliver and Sarah. "Oh. Wow." She kneaded her temple with the tips of her fingers. "The lobby doesn't seem like a good place to talk about this. Maybe you should come upstairs with me."

Aiden's assistant buzzed his extension. "Mr. Langford? Your sister is here to see you. She's brought a visitor."

Visitor? "Sure. Send them in." Aiden set aside the LangTel global marketing report he'd been skimming, easily the driest thing he'd ever read, which was saying a lot. With more than a dozen years in business under his belt, he'd digested his fair share of dull financial projections and legal briefs. He preferred to rely on his gut when making decisions. Billions later, the strategy had served him well.

In walked Anna with a blonde woman he didn't know. To say the stranger was eye catching would've been dismissive. With full pink lips and big blue eyes, wearing a black sundress, she was natural femininity embodied. Their gazes connected and he noticed the faintest of freckles dotting her cheeks. His tastes in women were wide and varied, but this woman ticked off more of his "yes" boxes than he cared to admit. Unfortunately, one thing about her made her absolutely not his type—the baby asleep in her arms. As a skilled avoider of emotional entanglements, moms were not on his list of women suitable for dating.

"Aiden, I want you to meet Sarah Daltrey," Anna said softly.

That name ended all thought of sexy sundresses and freckles. "You're the woman who keeps calling. You just called from the lobby. How in the world did you get to my sister?"

Anna shushed him. "The baby. He's sleeping."

The baby. His brain whirred into overdrive. He'd read Sarah's email. Well, one of them at least. That was enough to help him decide he shouldn't speak to her. He'd had false paternity accusations thrown at him before. When you have a vast fortune and come from a family well-known for success, you might as well have a target on your back. "This isn't right." His gut told him this was all wrong. "I don't know what Ms. Daltrey is after, but I'm calling security." He reached for the phone, but Anna clapped her hand over his.

"Aiden. Don't. Just listen. Please. It's important."

"I don't know what she's told you, but it's all lies." His pulse throbbed in his ears.

"Five minutes is all I ask, Mr. Langford." Sarah's voice suggested nothing less than calm professionalism. Not exactly the approach of someone unbalanced. But a baby? Oh, no. "If you don't believe me and what I came to tell you, you won't need to call security. I'll leave on my own."

Anna eyed her brother, asking his opinion with an arch of her eyebrows.

With pleas from two women who were obviously not going to give up, what choice did he have? "If it will put an end to this, then fine. Five minutes."

"I'll leave you two to it." Anna stopped at the door, turning to Sarah. "Stop by my office when you're done. I'd love to get the title of that book you mentioned about getting a baby to sleep through the night."

Sarah nodded and smiled as if she and Anna were best friends. What was he in for? "Yes, of course. Thanks so much for your help." The door clicked shut when Anna left, leaving behind a suffocating silence. Sarah cleared her throat and stepped closer, the baby's head still resting on her shoulder. "It would be great if I could sit. He's really heavy."

"Oh, sorry. Of course." Aiden offered a seat opposite his desk. He didn't know what he was supposed to do with himself—stand, sit, cross his arms. Nothing felt right, so he settled on his chair.

"I know this is strange," she started. "So I'll just get right to it. Oliver's mom was my best friend from high school. Her name was Gail Thompson. Does that ring a bell? She told me she met you at the Crowne Lotus Hotel in Bangkok."

Aiden's shoulders tightened. These tidbits of information hadn't been in Sarah's email. She'd only mentioned that she was guardian of his baby. To his knowledge, nobody knew about his brief affair with Gail. They'd met in the hotel bar and spent three days together before she went back to the US. That was the last he'd ever heard from her. "I do remember the name. Yes. But that doesn't mean anything." He shifted in his seat. He knew exactly where this was going. And that made his stomach lurch.

"Nine months after you and Gail had your little tryst in Thailand—" she fluttered her hand at him "—Oliver came along. Eight months after that, Gail called me and told me she had late stage cancer. I was the only person she could sign over guardianship to. She had no siblings— her parents died in a car accident when she was in college. She knew that I used to be a nanny and it just made sense. She said she tried to call you, but had even less luck than I did. It's hard to be persistent when you're dying."

Aiden swallowed hard. Sarah's email had mentioned that the baby's mom had fallen ill. He'd assumed that she was still alive and that this was a scam for money to pay medical bills. "She passed away?" An inexplicable tug came from the center of his chest as his vision drifted to the child. All alone in the world. He'd known that feeling well when he was young, and he despised the idea of any child growing up that way.

"Yes." Sarah pressed her lips together and nodded. She cupped the back of Oliver's head and kissed him softly on the cheek. "That left Oliver with no mom. I was left in charge of finding you so I can sign over guardianship. I think it'd be best for everyone if we kept this as simple as possible and try to wrap it up today."

Today? Did she say what I think she said? No. That was *not* happening. "You expect to waltz into my office, hand me a baby I've never seen in my life, and then what? You go back to wherever you came from and I'm expected to raise this child? I don't think so, Ms. Daltrey. You aren't going anywhere until I know for certain that the baby is mine. We need lawyers. Paternity tests. I'm not convinced this isn't a big fat hoax."

Her lips pressed into a thin line, but she otherwise seemed unfazed by his reaction. "First off, it's Sarah and his name is Oliver. And I understand you're shocked, but that's not my fault. If you'd taken my phone call, you could've been prepared for this."

"I seriously doubt I would've felt prepared. It's the middle of the workday. I'm a single man and an incredibly busy one at that. I am not prepared to care for a baby I didn't know about five minutes ago." Anger bubbled up inside him, but it was more than this inconceivable situation. He disliked his own dismissive tone. Considering the way his father had treated him, he didn't want to reject the little boy. No child deserved that. Especially one who didn't know who his father was.

"I understand you'll want a paternity test, but I think that the minute you see him awake, you'll realize he's yours. He looks just like you. Especially his eyes. Plus, he has the same birthmark you have on your upper thigh." A flush of pink colored her cheeks. She cast her eyes at her lap, seeming embarrassed. Despite the nature of their conversation, Aiden found it extremely charming. Sarah seemed to be the sort of person who wore her heart on her sleeve, a quality that made her incredibly sexy, too. "I mean, Gail told me you have one. And that's where Oliver gets it."

Sarah carefully hitched up the baby's pant leg. The child must've been incredibly tired—he hardly stirred when she revealed the mark. Aiden's breath caught in his throat. He rounded the desk, dropping down on one knee before them. He had to see it up close. He had to know this was real. The shape and size of the birthmark were indeed the same as his—an oval about the height of a dime, tilting to one side. The dark brown color was a match. *Is this possible?*

He reached out to touch the mark, but stopped himself. "I'm sorry. I'm a little taken aback."

"It's okay. He's your son." Sarah's voice was sweet and even. Given the impression he had of her from that first email, she was not at all the woman he'd envisioned.

The boy's skin was powdery soft and warm. Aiden gently tugged his pant leg back down, then studied his face. His eyelids were closed in complete relaxation, lined with dark lashes. His light brown hair had streaks of blond, admittedly much like Aiden's, although Oliver had baby-fine curls and Aiden's hair was straight and thick. Still, he knew from his own baby pictures that his hair had once been like Oliver's. Was this possible? Was this really happening? And what was he supposed to do about it? He had no idea how to care for a baby. This would change his entire life. Just when he was getting settled back in New York and trying to find a place for himself in his own family.

Oliver shifted in Sarah's arms, and for an instant, he opened his eyes and looked right at Aiden. The familiar flash of blue was a shot straight to Aiden's heart. It was like staring into a mirror. *Oh my God. He's mine.*

Two

Things weren't going terribly. Awkward, yes. Terrible, no.

It was really only awkward on Sarah's side of things. Aiden was still on bended knee watching Oliver sleep, and it was impossible not to stare at him. She tried to look elsewhere, to feign interest in the framed black-and-white photographs of exotic locales on his walls, or the view out his office window overlooking the Manhattan skyline, but she could only sustain it for a few moments. His blue eyes would draw her back in, so vivid and piercing she was sure he could hypnotize her if their gazes connected for more than a few heartbeats. They were topped by dark brows that suited his hard-nosed demeanor, accentuated by just a few tiny crinkles at the corners. The scruff on his face was a warm cinnamon brown, neatly tended, but gave him an edge that made her wonder what he was like when he wasn't so guarded. And there was something about the way he carried himself—more than self-assured, he came across as superhuman. Bulletproof. Sarah was certain Aiden Langford did precisely what he wanted to do, when and how he wanted to do it. He was not the sort of man who cared to be told what to do.

Too bad she had to do exactly that. The thought made her pulse race like an overcaffeinated jackrabbit. There was no telling how he would react, but judging by the look on his face, there was a chance it might go okay. However much of a handsome jerk he'd been when she walked in the door, his demeanor had softened in the last few minutes, ever since he'd taken a good look at Oliver. Surely he realized now, that even in the absence of hard evidence like the results of a paternity test, the baby was his.

"So," Sarah started, recalling the speech she'd practiced many times, words she dreaded saying because they would signal the end of her time with Oliver. "I was thinking that I'll leave Oliver with you now and I'll check into a hotel while we get this straightened out. A paternity test is a quick thing. We'll get your name on Oliver's birth certificate. I'll sign over the power of attorney and guardianship. All we need is a lawyer and a few days and then I can be out of your hair."

A crease formed in the center of Aiden's forehead as he stared at her. "Out of my hair?" It was just as tough to look into his eyes as she'd guessed it would be—they really were the spitting image of Oliver's. She'd fallen in love with that shade of blue over the last three weeks. "I already told you that you are not handing me a baby and walking away." He stood and straightened his charcoal suit jacket, which showed off his wide shoulders and broad frame. The way he loomed over her only accentuated his stature. There must've been something in the water in the Langford household—the two she'd met were ridiculously tall. "It seems to me that the more sensible course is for you to keep Oliver until this gets straightened out. You said it yourself—you used to be a nanny. You're used to caring for a child. I have zero experience in this area."

Of course, most single men, especially those who notoriously played the field, weren't in a position to drop everything and care for a baby. But Aiden Langford wasn't most men. Didn't he have a pile of money to throw at the problem? "I used to be a nanny. Past tense. That's no longer my vocation." She stopped short of admitting that she didn't have the stomach for it anymore. "You'll need to hire someone. I wrote down the number for the top nanny agency in the city for you. One phone call and they'll send someone over to help you."

"So I'm not only supposed to work with a complete stranger to take care of a baby, but the baby is supposed to accept that, too?"

He'd gone for the jugular with that one, although he seemed to be doing nothing more than making his case. The thought of anyone aside from his own father caring for Oliver made Sarah's chest, especially everything in the vicinity of her heart, seize up. "I'm a businesswoman, Mr. Langford. I need to return to Boston and my work."

"Business? What sort of business?" Although he was following the logical course of their conversation, Sarah couldn't help but bristle at his dismissive tone.

"I run a women's apparel company. It's really taking off. We can't even keep up with demand."

"Good problem to have. Until your vendors get tired of waiting and move on to something else."

Wasn't that the truth. Half of her day was spent reassuring boutique owners that their orders would be there soon. "That's exactly why I need to be back in Boston. And don't forget that I have been caring for *your* child full-time for nearly a month. It's time I go back to my life and let Oliver start his new one. With you." That last part had been particularly difficult to say, but the fact that her voice hadn't cracked only bolstered her confidence. She hadn't even shed a tear. It was a miracle.

Aiden sat on the edge of his desk and crossed his arms. His suit jacket sleeves drew taut across his muscles. How was she supposed to hold her own in an argument when he was distracting her with his physique? "So, I'll pay you for your time."

Ah, so he *did* know how to throw money at a problem. He was just lobbing it in the wrong direction. A breathy punch of a laugh left her lips. "I'm not for hire."

"I'll pay you double whatever your going rate used to be."

She huffed.

"Fine. Triple."

"You're a terrible negotiator."

He shrugged. "I do what's necessary to get what I want."

"That would make me the most expensive nanny in the history of child care. I was paid very well for my services. I was very good at my job."

"You're only making my argument for me. Money is no object, Ms. Daltrey. If Oliver really is my son, he deserves the best. Sounds to me like that's you."

She shook her head. "No way. Absolutely not." This was not the way this was supposed to go. She needed to put an end to Aiden Langford and his money-throwing, muscle-bulging ways.

Oliver fussed and rubbed his eyes, moving his head fitfully as he woke.

Sarah had spoken too loudly. Nap time was apparently now over. She stood and attempted to hand the baby to Aiden. "Here. Take your son. At least for a minute."

Oliver refused, clinging to Sarah.

"See? He clearly wants to be with you. I'm a stranger to him. Would you really leave a baby with a stranger?"

She pursed her lips, calculating her best response. Of course she wouldn't do that. But after the extensive research she'd done on Aiden, he didn't really seem like a stranger. That, however, was not information she cared to share. Which meant she was back at nothing.

"Even worse," he continued. "A stranger who doesn't know how to change a diaper, or what to feed him, or what to do if he starts to cry."

"No idea? I know you have two younger siblings. You never babysat?"

Aiden threaded his fingers through his hair, tousling it in the process. "No."

Well, shoot. She couldn't hand over Oliver to a man he didn't know, especially not one who might not be able to care for him, even if that had been her plan. Her horribly simple plan. "I don't think it's a good idea for me to take Oliver to a hotel, either. He needs to get used to being with you. And you're apparently going to need to learn how to take care of him."

"Excuse me if I haven't thought it out quite that far yet. This is still a new concept for me." He blew out a breath, seeming deep in thought. "I guess the thing that makes the most sense is for you both to stay with me. Until we get things straightened out. And I can hire a nanny. I guess I have to buy a crib, too? I mean, really, this is a lot to pile on a person in one day."

He wasn't wrong. Maybe it would be in Oliver's best interest if she stayed for a couple of days, even if it would make it exponentially more difficult to say good-bye to him. As for the to-do list to get Aiden up and running with the baby, it was a long one if she was going to be thorough. They would need time. With the bad hand Oliver had been dealt in life, she owed it to him to spend a few days in New York so he could be off to the best possible start with Aiden. That was exactly what she'd promised Gail. "Okay. We'll stay at your place."

"You'll have to tell me what you want to be paid. I have no earthly idea how much money a nanny makes. Or even what a nanny does, other than everything a parent would do if they were around."

She'd first said no to Aiden's money on principle, but

if she was going to help him with Oliver, she could get something from him that was far more valuable than a paycheck. She knew from her online snooping that he was a whiz when it came to growing companies. It was in his blood—the Langfords were one of the most successful entrepreneurial families in US history. Maybe he could help her solve the countless problems she was facing with trying to take her business to the next level.

"I don't want your money. I want your expertise."

"I'm listening." He cocked an eyebrow at her, threatening to make her throat close up.

"Business expertise. I want you to help me with my company. Help me find investors. Help me figure out my manufacturing issues and widen my distribution."

He nodded, clearly calculating. "That's a tall order. Between that and me going through baby school, this is going to take more than a few days. We'll need at least a week. At least."

How long could she do this? Every minute with Oliver only made her love him more. She clutched him, kissed his head, taking in his sweet baby smell. *We don't have to say goodbye today, buddy. I guess that much is good.* "Today is Friday. I'll give you ten days. I teach you how to care for Oliver. You help me with my company."

"I think I'd be a fool to say no. You have me in a corner here."

"I mean it, though. Ten days and I'm out of here."

"Like I said. In a corner."

"Okay, then. I want to have a say in the nanny you hire, too. And I want to help outfit the nursery."

Aiden then did the last thing she ever expected. He smiled. Not a lot, just enough to create the tiniest crack in his facade. Sarah felt as if she'd had the wind knocked out of her. His face lit up, especially his eyes. "Anything else?"

"That's all for now."

"Just so you know, fashion is outside my realm of expertise. Women's clothing isn't really my world."

Ah, but he hadn't let her finish. Given Aiden Langford's reputation for being a ladies' man, she had no doubt that he was well-versed in her specialty. "Actually, it's women's sleepwear and lingerie. Something tells me you know at least a little something about that."

Three

Oliver in her arms, Sarah climbed out of Aiden's black SUV, squinting behind sunglasses at the apartment building before them. About a dozen stories high, it had an antique brick facade blanketed in tidy sections of ivy and dotted with tall leaded glass windows. This was not what she'd envisioned for Aiden Langford's abode. She'd assumed a high-rise overlooking Central Park. Wasn't that his birthright? Ritzy address and an equally swanky apartment? Instead, he resided on Fifth Avenue at Twenty-sixth Street, in the Flatiron District with a view of Madison Square Park. She had a sneaking suspicion that Aiden was full of surprises. And that this was the first of many.

"Is that one yours?" She pointed at the highest floor. "The one on top with the biggest terrace?"

Aiden wheeled Sarah's suitcase from the car, lugging the teddy bear that was easily twice Oliver's size, while Aiden's driver John unloaded the remaining bags of toys and baby clothes. "The top four floors are my apartment."

Sarah gulped, surveying the manicured spaces—a formal balcony with stone columns and wrought iron on the lowest level all the way up to one that looked like a park in its own right, each spanning the building. He'd still gone for swanky, merely in a different corner of the city. "That's a lot of room for a single guy."

"My third floor is empty. And the fourth floor is all outdoors. I need my space."

"I'm surprised you don't live up by Anna and her husband. She was telling me she lives only a few minutes from your mom."

Aiden cast his sights down at her, his sunglasses revealing nothing but her own reflection. The crinkles in his forehead and the way his brows drew together were enough indication that he didn't like the question. The driver slammed the car tailgate. Sarah jumped.

"Like I said, I need my space." Aiden's voice was stern, like a father telling his wayward teenage daughter that she'd better be home before eleven.

Okay, then. Dropping the subject.

Together, they entered the beautifully appointed lobby. Black-and-white-checkerboard marble floors and a chandelier dripping with crystals hinted at both wealth and good taste. Sarah pushed Oliver in the stroller while she tried to remember to take deep breaths. Everything about this made her heart beat an uneven rhythm—

entering into an agreement with a man she hardly knew, staying in his home, handing over the little boy she'd already grown to love more than she'd thought possible. She did everything she could to ignore the feeling in the pit of her stomach, the one saying that each passing minute was another step away from what she was supposed to be doing—leaving nannying behind, once and for all.

Stop being negative. This is good for Oliver. She had to believe that. Really, it was the best scenario for him—a transition period where his new dad could become acquainted with parenting. They'd find a nanny, set up the nursery. In ten days, this sweet little boy would be given the best possible start at a new life. And she'd get back to hers in Boston, a simple and solitary existence with its own rewards, the most notable of which was the chance to pursue a career that didn't leave her so open to heartbreak.

They stepped onto the elevator and Sarah closed her eyes to ward off her claustrophobia. Plus, every time she looked at Aiden, he got to her with his all-knowing gaze. No wonder the man had such a reputation with the ladies. Most women were probably too mesmerized by his penetrating stare to entertain a single lucid thought beyond, *Of course, Aiden. Whatever you want, Aiden.*

The elevator dinged, and John, loaded down with the bulk of the baby supplies, held the door for Sarah as she wheeled Oliver off the elevator. They entered a stunning foyer with glossy wood floors, an exotic carved console table and several colorful abstract paintings. Aiden followed with his laptop bag, Sarah's suitcase and the teddy bear, which was a nice counterpoint to his tailored gray suit and midnight-blue tie.

"Where would you like these, Mr. Langford?" John asked.

"Just leave them here. I'm not entirely sure where everything is going yet."

John did as instructed, neatly placing the bags on the table.

"Thank you so much for the help. I really appreciate it," Sarah said to John.

He turned and looked at her as if she had a unicorn horn sprouting from her forehead. "It's my job, ma'am."

"Well, we came with a lot of stuff. I'm sure Mr. Langford doesn't normally make you lug stuffed animals and diaper bags."

"I'm happy to do it. But thank you. For saying thank you." He smiled warmly.

Aiden watched the back and forth. "That's it for now, John. I'll let you know if I need anything else."

"I'll be downstairs, Mr. Langford." John stepped onto the elevator and the doors slid closed.

"He's really nice," Sarah said. "We talked quite a bit while we were figuring how to get the car seat into the SUV. He told me all about his wife and kids. Good guy."

"Of course. A very good guy." Everything in Aiden's voice said that he didn't know the first thing about his driver, and that it quite possibly had never occurred to him to ask.

"Now what?" Sarah wanted Aiden to take the lead. His house. His baby.

"Tell me why a baby needs a stuffed animal this large."

Sarah shrugged, unsubtly peeking ahead at what she could see of the apartment, which seemed to stretch on for days. "Kids love to have things to snuggle with. And eventually, Oliver will be bigger than the bear."

"Ah. I see."

"You'll learn."

"I have a feeling I won't have a choice." Aiden leaned her small suitcase against the wall and propped the bear up on top of it. "And how did you get all of this onto a train, then off a train and into the city, all by yourself?"

"Let's just say that I relied on the kindness of strangers. And I'm a very good tipper. I managed."

"You're resourceful. I'll give you that much."

Sarah went to get Oliver out of his stroller, but decided it was time to start the learning process. "Aiden. Here. You unbuckle him and get him out."

"You sure? I don't have the first clue what I'm doing."

"You have to start somewhere."

Aiden crouched down and Oliver messed with his hair while Aiden tried to decipher the maze of straps and buckles. Sarah watched, not wanting to interfere. Oliver was doing enough on his own, tugging on Aiden's jacket and kicking him in the chest.

Aiden sat back on his haunches, raking his hair from his face. "Is he always like this? So full of energy and into everything?"

"Unless he's asleep, yes. Now pick him up."

Aiden threaded his massive hands under the baby's tiny arms, lifting him as if he might break him if he went too fast, then holding Oliver awkwardly against his torso.

"Bend your arm and let him sit in the crook of your elbow." Sarah shifted Oliver into position. She straightened Aiden's suit coat while she was at it. She stood back and admired the change. The strong, strapping man holding her favorite baby on the planet was awfully sexy. "See? That wasn't so bad."

Oliver leaned toward Sarah, holding out his arms for her.

"I think he wants to be with you."

Sarah had to be firm. "He'll be fine. He needs to be with you. Let's start the tour so we can start planning the nursery. He'll stay in your arms if we're busy and there are things to look at."

Aiden blew out a breath and they strolled into the modern, open apartment. The space had very high ceilings and was decorated almost exclusively in white, black and gray. Everything was meticulous and neat, just like Aiden's office at LangTel. He was in for a big wake-up call when Oliver took over and there were toys everywhere. Best not to mention that, though. He'd learn.

To her right was a massive gourmet kitchen with an eight-burner stove and seating for six at the center island. Beyond the kitchen, she could see a hint of a dining room tucked away, then a staircase, and beyond that a room with a sofa and the beautiful windows she'd noticed on the front of the building. As a nanny, Sarah had seen grand displays of money, but nothing that hinted at this level of affluence. Although she was no real estate agent, the house had to be at least five thousand square feet if the other floors were the same size. By comparison, her Boston apartment probably could've fit inside the kitchen. When Aiden had said he needed his space, he wasn't kidding.

"The living room is at the front of the building, overlooking the park."

"Beautiful. Absolutely stunning." Sarah followed as Aiden led them in the opposite direction.

"This is the library." He nodded to his right, where black, open-back bookcases delineated the room. The shelves were packed with books. "The room with the French doors at the back of the building is my home office."

Aiden did a one-eighty and Sarah trailed behind him, past the dining room and stairs, to the living room. It was a grand and comfortable space with charcoal-gray sectional couches, a flat-screen TV above a stacked stone fireplace and a massive glass coffee table. "Another beautiful room."

"Thank you." He shifted Oliver in his arms, seeming ever-so-slightly more comfortable with holding him.

"Unfortunately, we're going to need to babyproof in here like nobody's business."

"Why? What's wrong with it?"

Sarah didn't know where to start. "There are outlets everywhere. The coffee table is a disaster waiting to happen. I can just see Oliver bonking his head. You'll probably have to put up a gate to keep him away from the fireplace. As for the rest of the house, that's going to need an overhaul, too. Those stairs will need a gate, too."

"Isn't that how children learn? By making mistakes?" There was no misconstruing the annoyance in his voice.

"Not on my watch, they don't. At least not the kind of mistakes that put a child in the emergency room."

A low grumble left his throat. "Talk about turning my entire life upside down." He shook his head and took what seemed like his hundredth deep breath. "I'll need you to make a list. We'll tackle it that way."

"Not a normal nanny responsibility, but okay."

"I thought you weren't a nanny anymore."

"I'm not."

"Well then. This is part of our business arrangement. You need my expertise. I need yours."

"Fine." Sarah walked over to a long, dark wood console table against the wall, plopping her handbag down to dig out a piece of paper. A handful of framed photographs were directly above—one taken from the viewpoint of someone skydiving, one looking straight down the side of a cliff with a waterfall and jungle in the periphery, and another of a group of men and donkeys on a narrow path carved into a mountainside. Each looked like something out of a movie. "Nice pictures. Are these from *National Geographic*?"

"Remembrances of my adventures."

"Wait. What? These are yours?"

Aiden nodded, fighting a smile. He joined her, Oliver in tow. Aiden was doing well with the baby, and she was happy to see him master his first few moments of dad duty. "I enjoy pushing the limits," he said.

Goose bumps cropped up on Sarah's arms. A man with a dangerous side held mysterious appeal, probably because it was the opposite of her personality. She'd fallen for a few guys who liked to live on the edge over the years. None of them was good at flexing their bravado in the realm of relationships.

"You're going to have to set aside your daredevil escapades for a little while. Skydiving is not an approved activity for a toddler."

He scowled. "I'm not enjoying this part, in case you're wondering. The part where you tell me how I have to construct my life around someone else's needs."

She patted him on the shoulder. "Welcome to parenthood. It's good for you. It'll remind you that the world doesn't revolve around you."

"Jumping out of an airplane reminds me that I'm still alive," Aiden countered. "And that I'd better find a way to enjoy my time on this planet."

There was a somber hint to that last string of words, but she was still piecing together who and what Aiden Langford truly was. It struck her as sad that he lived all alone in this big house, however much it was a showplace. Despite his protestations, Sarah couldn't imagine Oliver as anything less than a blessing in Aiden's life, quite possibly his salvation.

Oliver reached for the pictures, pointing to the skydiving snapshot. Aiden stepped close enough for him to touch it.

"Pretty cool, huh? I took that picture. I jumped out of an airplane. Maybe you and I can do that someday. Someday when Sarah isn't around to tell us what to do."

Oliver turned to Aiden, concentrating hard on his face. He flattened his palm against Aiden's cheek.

Aiden reached up and covered Oliver's hand with his, a fascinated smile crossing his face. A sweet and tender moment, it left Sarah on the verge of tears. For the first time since she'd gotten off the train that afternoon, she was less worried about Aiden accepting fatherhood. They weren't out of the woods, but he was already showing signs of folding Oliver into his life. Which meant one step closer to Sarah being out of it.

Oliver needs his father. His new family. "For now, I still get to tell you what to do, at least when it comes to Oliver. I say it's time to find him a bedroom in this massive house of yours."

Aiden walked Sarah and Oliver up to the second floor, holding the little boy. He was slowly growing comfortable with this tiny human clutching the lapel of his suit coat, keeping him warm and reacting to the world Aiden walked through every day without giving it a second thought. It all was new to Oliver—sights and sounds, people and places. He didn't play the role of stranger though; he played explorer, full of curiosity. Aiden had to admire that disposition. He was cut from the same cloth.

They reached the top of the stairs and the hall where all four bedrooms were. At the far end was his master suite. There was only one other room furnished, for guests. The other two remained unused and unoccupied. With most of his family in the city, visitors weren't common, nor would they likely ever be. His friends, small in number and much like him in that they preferred to roam the globe, were not prone to planning a visit. No, the apartment with arguably too much space for a confirmed bachelor had been purchased with one thing in mind—breathing room.

He fought the sense that Sarah and Oliver were encroaching on his refuge. He made accommodations for no one and doing so put him on edge, but it was about more than covering electrical outlets and putting up gates. He hadn't come close to wrapping his head around his newfound fatherhood, even if he did accept that with the arrival of Sarah Daltrey, everything had changed.

He was counting on the results of the paternity test to help it all sink in. He'd already made the call to his lawyer. It would mean a lot to know that Oliver was truly his. Aiden had lived much of his own life convinced that Roger and Evelyn Langford—the people he called his parents—had lied to him about who Aiden's father was. Roger Langford's death nearly a year ago had made the uncertainty even more painful and the truth that much more elusive. He wasn't about to badger his mother, a grieving widow, over his suspicions. But he would confront her, eventually. He couldn't mend fences with his family until that much was known, and there was a lot of mending to be done. Aiden had made his own mistakes, too. Big, vengeful mistakes.

"I was thinking we could put Oliver in here." Aiden showed one of the spare rooms to Sarah. "It's the biggest. I mean, he is going to get bigger, isn't he?" Talk about things he hadn't considered…life beyond today, when Oliver would be older…preschool, grade school and beyond. No matter what, Aiden didn't need to think about where Oliver would go to school. He would be wherever Aiden was. There would be no shipping him off as his parents had done to him.

"Is it the closest room to yours?" Sarah asked.

"No. The smallest is the closest."

"That's probably a better choice for now." Without invitation, she ventured farther down the hall. "In here?" Sarah strolled in and turned in the small, but bright space—not much more than four walls and a closet. "This is better. It'll make it easier on you. He still gets up in the middle of the night."

"And I'll need to get up with him." He stated it rather than framing it as a question. He was prepared to do anything to feel less out of his element, as if any of this were logical to him, which it wasn't.

Oliver fussed and kicked, wanting to get down.

"Let's let him crawl around," Sarah said.

Aiden gently placed the little boy on the floor. He took off like a bolt of lightning, scrambling all over the room on his hands and knees.

Sarah pulled a few toys out of her bag and offered them to Oliver. "Yes. You'll need to get up with him and comfort him, especially when he's teething like he is now."

Aiden leaned against the door frame, acting as a barrier in case Oliver decided to escape. "Is that why he drools so much?"

Sarah smiled and sat on the floor with Oliver, tucking her legs beneath her, her dress flounced around her. "My mother used to say that's not drool. It's the sugar melting."

Aiden wasn't prone to smiling, let alone laughing, at things that were quaint and homey. But he couldn't have stopped if he'd wanted to. He drank in the vision of Sarah. She was so different from every woman he'd ever known. She was beautiful, but not made up. Eloquent, but not pretentious. There was no hidden agenda, nor did she seem concerned with impressing him. She just came right out with it, but didn't mow people over with her ideas. She simply stated what she found to be best, in a manner that made it seem as if it were the only logical choice.

Sarah again looked around the room. "We should probably order a crib online and see how quickly we can have it delivered, along with some other necessities. He'll need a dresser, a changing table. You should probably invest in a rocking chair for this room." She began counting on her fingers. "Then there's clothes, diapers, formula, bottles, toys, bath supplies, baby laundry detergent."

"Special laundry detergent?"

Pressing her lips together, she nodded. "When he's crying in the middle of the night, you don't want to be wondering if it's because his skin is irritated. One less thing to worry about."

Just when he thought he was getting a handle on things, a new spate of information came down the pike. "Like I said before, it'd be great if you could make some lists. You can use the computer in my home office and get a lot of that ordered."

"We need to call the nanny agency, too. They probably don't take calls after five on a Friday. Sounds like we have a busy night ahead of us. Oliver's going to need a bath, too." Oliver crawled over to Sarah with a stuffed toy in his hand and showed it to her.

Aiden's cell phone rang with a call from his sister Anna. "Excuse me for a minute. I need to make sure this isn't anything important."

"Sure thing. I'll call the nanny agency and Oliver can play. Avoiding outlets, of course."

"Right. The outlets." *Gotta deal with that, ASAP.* He accepted the call and stepped out into the hall. "Anna, hi. Everything okay?"

"I was calling to ask you the same thing. Is everything going well with Sarah and Oliver? I can't believe it, Aiden. A baby. It's so amazing. Are you just bursting at the seams?"

Aiden wandered into his room and sat on the leather bench at the foot of the bed. "More like my brain is about to implode. I don't know what I'm supposed to feel. At least you've had time to get used to the idea of becoming a parent. It's only been a few hours for me."

"I'm sure it will take some time, but I'm so excited for you. You know, the minute I looked into Oliver's eyes, I knew he was yours. He looks just like you. It's going to blow Mom's mind when she sees him."

Oh no. The one thing he hadn't yet taken into account. "Please tell me you haven't said anything to Mom. Or Adam for that matter, but especially not Mom. I need to figure out how best to deal with this."

"I haven't said a peep."

He exhaled a little too loudly, if only to make the weight of dealing with his mother subside. "Good."

His mind often raced at the mere mention of his mom, thoughts quickly mired in bad memories and sad stories. He couldn't fathom the moment when she'd meet the son he hadn't known he had. Would he feel better about his suspicions, a misgiving he'd shared with no one other than Anna? Or would he feel worse? Either way, his mother's reaction to Oliver would be telling. If she accepted him unconditionally, he'd always wonder why she hadn't treated him the same way. If she rejected him, he'd have a hard time not blowing up at her.

"When are you going to tell her?" Anna asked.

"Tomorrow. Or maybe Sunday. I need time to get us settled." He rested his elbows on his knees. "Sarah's calling the nanny agency, we have an entire nursery of furniture to order and I'm apparently in Daddy School after that. I have to learn how to change a diaper and give him a bath."

Anna tittered.

"What's so funny?"

"I like the image of you bathing a baby. It's sweet. And unlike anything I ever imagined you doing."

"You and me both. I never thought I'd have kids." *Not after everything with Dad.*

"Sometimes life gives us unexpected gifts. I felt like that when I got pregnant."

Anna was carrying a miracle baby. Her doctor had told her it would be nearly impossible to conceive and even more difficult to carry a pregnancy to term, but she was doing great. "I hear you. I'm still getting used to it."

"Well, promise me you won't keep Oliver to yourself. I want to see him, too. I could even come over and take care of him if you need help. I could bring Jacob. It would be great practice for us."

Anna always managed to take the edge off his greatest concerns. Even if he'd come back to New York and everything had been a total disaster with the rest of his family, he still would've forged a better relationship with Anna. "Thanks. I'll definitely need your help after Sarah leaves."

"She's staying for ten whole days? How'd you convince her to do that? She seemed hell-bent on only being in town through the weekend when we first talked."

"We made a deal. She gives me ten days and I help her with her business." Aiden then realized that his sister might be able to help. Before she'd taken a job at Lang-Tel, she'd been CFO for a company that manufactured women's workout clothes. "Did Sarah happen to tell you what she does?"

"She did. And the idea of you helping her with it is almost as amusing as the image of you giving Oliver a bath."

"I'm glad you find my life changes so entertaining right now. Do you think you could help me out with some contacts in the garment industry? I haven't talked to Sarah about it that much, but I know she needs manufacturing and warehousing and distribution. Maybe you know someone I could call."

"Oh, absolutely. Let me think about it and I'll email you a list."

"Perfect." One thing he could check off his to-do list. "God only knows how I'll get any work done on Monday when I'm back at the office. I doubt I'll get much rest this weekend."

"Don't worry about that. Work can wait. You're a dad now. That's the most important thing."

Four

Sitting on the floor in Oliver's room, Sarah ended her call with the nanny agency. She leaned down and kissed the baby's head. He'd been playing quietly in her lap for a few minutes. "Guess what? Your daddy's going to hire someone very nice to take care of you. Won't that be great?"

Oliver gnawed on a plastic teething ring, not interested in much else.

Sarah swept his soft curls to the side. "She'll play with you and take you for walks in the park and sing songs to you. Just like I do." Her voice wobbled as Oliver peeked up at her with wide eyes. She wrinkled her nose and forced herself to smile, if only to stop tears from gathering. The thought of leaving Oliver was as unhappy as it was inevitable. Getting attached to children who weren't her own was no longer part of her self-destructive pattern. Nor was getting wrapped up in the life of a single dad. The sooner she left Oliver with Aiden, the better.

"It really is too bad that you can't just stay and be his nanny," Aiden said.

Sarah nearly fainted. First out of surprise at his voice, then from the view as she slanted her sights to him. Leaning against the door frame, he stood there like he could hold up the whole world that way. He'd changed clothes. In a long-sleeved black T-shirt and a pair of jeans with a dark wash, he was now at a level of casual she hadn't pondered, although he had to take off the suit at some point. That thought sent her brain skipping ahead, especially now that she could better see the contours of his shoulders and how well-defined his chest was. No doubt about it—Aiden Langford logged his fair share of time in the gym.

Cut it out. The things cycling through her mind were not good—thoughts of peeling away his T-shirt and smoothing her hands over his chest, kissing him. Her curiosity was getting the best of her, and his presence was making it worse. Unfortunately, his expression was just as irresistible as the rest of the package—a look that said he didn't care what anyone else thought about, well, anything. Sarah could hardly keep her jaw in a place that suggested some measure of decorum. Forget ladylike—right now she was going for not ogling him like a sex-starved loon.

"I adore Oliver, but I told you I'm no longer a nanny."

Aiden stepped into the room and once again, something about the way he moved left her pulse unsettled. He held up his hands in surrender. "Got it. No more nannying for you. But did you call the service?"

"I did. They'll send candidates over on Monday morning. We can sit down before then and go over your priorities. And mine, of course."

"We? You know, I'm more than capable of conducting an interview. And you aren't going to have to put up with this person. I am."

She narrowed her focus on him. "You asked for my help." She stood and gathered Oliver in her arms, settling him on her hip. "Some of these nannies will embellish on their experience just to get the primo jobs. I'll see past that."

"This is one of those primo jobs?"

"With this house? Yes. And you're going to need someone at your beck and call with your schedule. I told them you need live-in help." Sarah didn't like this idea, although she couldn't arrive at a sensible reason why. She only knew that the myth of the nanny falling for the father of her charge was very real. It happened all the time. It had happened to her. If Aiden were to be judged on his looks alone, she could see most women falling for him. Add in the money, power and semi-arrogant veneer? Forget it. It was only a matter of time.

"Wait a minute. I'm not just getting one new member of the household, I'm getting two? Can't the nanny live at her house and come over when I go to work?"

"That might work if you had a backup, like a family member. Otherwise, I can't imagine you waiting for the nanny to show up so you can go to work. What about your mom?"

Lightning fast, Aiden plucked Oliver from her arms. "My mother will not be taking care of him."

Sarah grappled with his hyperprotective reaction. A few hours ago, he'd been ready to banish her and the baby from LangTel corporate headquarters forever. Now, there was something else to contend with, something that Sarah sensed went deep. "Why? Most people would do anything to have a grandparent around to care for their child."

"Not me."

"Technically, I'm Oliver's legal guardian. I have a right to know why." None of this added up. Aiden's sister Anna had spoken warmly of her mother. Sarah had read about Evelyn Langford when she was researching Aiden. She sat on countless charity boards and was known for her generosity with children's hospitals, cancer research and battered women's shelters. By all reports, her benevolence had grown in the wake of her husband's death.

"I'm not saying my mother would hurt him. Not that. It's…" He closed his eyes for a moment and Sarah's breath hitched in her throat. No air would go in, nor would it come out. She was too in awe of this glimpse of vulnerability. It was so incongruous with his personality. He was showing a different side of himself, a side Sarah wanted to know. A side Sarah wanted to comfort. "It's complicated. Let's just say that for now, it's best if you know that my mother can't be relied upon for anything."

There was a finality to his tone that said Sarah should leave it alone. "Okay."

"What's the schedule for the rest of the night? I have some work I need to tend to."

Sarah consulted her phone—nearly five o'clock. "Oliver eats at five thirty. Bath time at six o'clock, story time at six forty-five. Bedtime is at seven."

"Is that Oliver's schedule or yours?"

"It's everybody's schedule. That's how things work with a baby. It makes him feel secure. He knows what happens and when."

It was impossible to ignore Aiden's attitude. Once again, he seemed put out. "I see. I guess I still have a lot to learn. We can order some takeout to come for us around eight. I trust that will work?"

She nodded. "Yes. That will give us the perfect time to talk about my business." There had to be some payoff for allowing herself to get in deeper, when she'd told herself she'd never do that.

"I spoke to my sister Anna about it briefly. She may be able to help. I wasn't kidding when I told you that I don't have many connections in that business. I can't promise you the world."

But you can ask the world of me. She stopped before the words left her lips, but she was all too familiar with handsome, powerful men who expected everything for very little in return. "Well, if nothing else, I'm sure you can give me some good advice. That alone could end up being very helpful."

"Come on. Let's go down to my office and we'll get the nursery furniture ordered."

They headed downstairs and Aiden led them to the double French doors, into one of the coziest, most gorgeous rooms Sarah had ever seen. The office had a different feel to it than the rest of the house, warmer and more colorful. The walls were a deep navy, and an ornate Oriental carpet sat in the center of the room, topped with a pair of club chairs and a massive oak desk. Bookshelves lined two of the walls from floor to ceiling.

"More books? Even with the home library?"

Aiden shrugged and rounded to the chocolate-brown leather desk chair. "I like to read. It's a nice escape."

"Escape? From what?"

"Excuse me?"

"From where I sit, you have a pretty perfect life. You have this gorgeous home, a job that tons of people would kill for and you don't seem to be hurting from the financial end of things. More than anything, you don't seem to do anything you don't want to do. At all. Ever."

For a moment, he just glared, not saying a word. He wasn't angry, nor was he pleased. "You say whatever you want to say, don't you?"

"It's not that bizarre a question. I've seen the pictures. Skydiving. Hiking the Andes. I'm just wondering what you need to escape from."

"Stress," he answered flatly, methodically spinning a pen on a pad of paper. She hadn't noticed his hands much before now and she was kicking herself for not paying better attention. His fingers moved gracefully, demonstrating their ability to do things deftly, but they were manly, too—strong. Able.

"Stress." Her stupid brain leaped ahead to methods

of reducing stress and none of it had to do with reading. Again she was knee-deep in thoughts of what he looked like under that T-shirt.

"Yes." He opened his laptop and placed his fingers on the keyboard, but stopped before typing. "I don't even know where to start. Do I just search for baby crib?"

"Here. Let me do it." She carried Oliver around behind Aiden's desk and handed him the baby. Oliver settled in on Aiden's lap, but reached for the pen.

"Can I let him have this?"

"No. He'll put it in his mouth. You can run upstairs and grab a toy out of his room."

Aiden raised an eyebrow as if she'd made the most ludicrous suggestion ever.

She shrugged and waved him off. "Gotta start being Daddy sometime. Now shoo. Let me see what I can find online."

Aiden trekked out of the office with Oliver. Sarah rested her chin on her hand, watching as they made their way down the straight shot of the house, past the library and the kitchen, until they disappeared up the stairs. Aiden was so big, Oliver so tiny in his arms. She hoped to hell they would be okay on Sunday, after she left. She couldn't bear the thought of anything else.

She pulled up a browser window and quickly found a furniture place offering next day delivery in Manhattan. That was the genius part of being in a big city. Virtually anything could be delivered at any time. Once she was done, a delivery truck would be set to arrive in front of Aiden's building tomorrow morning. And she'd be one step closer to removing herself from Aiden's and Oliver's life.

Five

Aiden had learned one thing already—fatherhood was no walk in the park. He'd struggled through his first attempt at feeding Oliver his dinner. With no high chair, they'd had to improvise by wheeling Oliver's stroller into the dining room. The baby rubbed his eyes and turned his head, refusing every spoonful Aiden offered. He had to hand it to Sarah, though—she only gave advice when asked. She'd otherwise sat by quietly and watched as a man capable of orchestrating billion-dollar deals and negotiating with cantankerous CEOs was unable to convince a fussy toddler to take a single bite of food. Frustrated, he'd finally asked her to do it. She took over, Oliver downing an entire jar of baby food with hardly a single complaint. Aiden walked away from the dinner table with a bruised ego. And baby food on his jeans.

He wasn't sure what to make of bath time, either. But this time, Sarah took charge.

"This is the only tub you have in the house?"

Aiden failed to understand the question. The tub was perfect, in that it fit two people. For him, seduction was the only reason to get in a bathtub. "Yes. What's wrong with it?"

"It's huge."

"Of course it is. It's a two-person soaking tub." He cleared his throat, waiting for her next comment.

"Well, you're going to have to get in there with him. I refuse to bathe a child in the kitchen sink. It's not sanitary."

He turned and dropped his head until his chin was nearly flat against his chest. He was at least a foot taller than her, maybe more, and they were nearly toe-to-toe. She was still wearing the sundress from earlier in the day. Had that really been today? So much had happened, it was hard to wrap his brain around it. "So you're going to see me naked before we've known each other for eight hours? You take things quickly."

"Very funny. No, Oliver gets to get naked. You're putting on swim trunks. If I had a bathing suit with me, I'd do it myself. But I don't, and you need to bond with him."

He raised an eyebrow. "This from the woman who swore I'd have no problem feeding him dinner."

She shrugged. "Babies are unpredictable. The sooner you learn that, the better. I promise you that physical contact will help you and Oliver to bond. It's a scientific fact. Now go change. I'll get the water running."

"I like it hot."

"You'll get lukewarm and like it."

He grumbled, but made his way into his walk-in closet, closing the door behind him. He took off his clothes and plucked a pair of board shorts from the bottom drawer of his bureau, slipping into them and tying the white string at the waist. He opened the door. "Ready."

Sarah turned, glancing at him over her shoulder. Every muscle in his body tightened from that single flash of her eyes and the immediate connection he felt. Good God she was gorgeous, all deep blue eyes and skin flushed with rosy pink. She shied away. "So I see."

He liked getting that reaction. He liked it a lot. "What now?"

"Get in. I'll hand him to you." She tended to Oliver, who was pulling himself to standing at the edge of the bathtub. He bounced up and down on his toes while Sarah took off his pants and diaper.

"He seems excited."

"Just you wait. He loves bath time. It's a good thing you're in your trunks. I'm going to get soaked."

Aiden climbed into the tub, wrestling with the idea of Sarah, soaked, and the white-hot image it conjured. Sure, they only had ten days together, but that was plenty of time for him. In fact, it was his preference—a strict, short timetable. But was that a good idea? From a physical standpoint, sure. From every other standpoint, he didn't know. There were repercussions and awkward conversations to worry about. *Dammit.*

Sarah handed him the baby and he let Oliver sit on

his lap while he wrapped his hands around his waist. The baby wasted no time slapping the surface of the water and sending it flying.

Sarah laughed and dropped a few plastic toys into the bath. "Told you."

Splash splash splash. Oliver looked at Sarah, who beamed at him as if she couldn't be any more in love with someone if she tried. She rested her elbows on the edge of the tub and leaned closer, flicking at the water with the tips of her fingers. Oliver giggled, then mimicked her in a far less delicate way. *Splash splash splash.* He laughed so hard his entire body shook. It was impossible not to find the fun in their game, even with water being flung at his face and shoulders, not to mention all over the bathroom.

"Is bath time always this chaotic?"

"Basically. Anything you can do to get him clean. And it helps relax him."

Splash splash splash. Another peal of Oliver's sweet giggles rang out.

"It relaxes him?"

"Believe it or not, yes. He has a lot of energy. This helps to get it out." Sarah pulled out a toiletry bag and poured a dollop of golden shampoo into her hand. "Get his hair wet. We don't have a cup, so just use your hands."

Aiden scooped water with one hand, curling his arm around wiggly Oliver. He started tentatively, unsure if the baby would like it, but quickly learned that he took no issue with water running down his face. Aiden had a little fish on his hands. How amazing it would be to teach him to swim, then snorkel and surf, another of Aiden's favorite pastimes. *Small waves at first. It's dangerous.* He was still getting used to these parental thoughts, but he was amazed how quickly they had kicked in. Especially when the topic of his mother had come up. He hadn't meant to impulsively take Oliver out of Sarah's arms. He only knew that was his gut talking—and reacting. Oliver would know nothing but unconditional love from his family. He wasn't certain his mother could offer it, and until she'd demonstrated as much, she would be kept on a very short leash.

Sarah leaned over and shampooed Oliver's head, his blond curls becoming matted and soapy. A soft fragrance filled the air.

"It smells nice," he said.

"It smells like baby, and that's the most wonderful smell in the world. Well, most of the time. There are times when it gets stinky, too."

"I bet." Like most things, there would be both good and bad to parenting. Aiden was optimistic about more good, mostly because he and Oliver had a clean slate. Aiden would not do to Oliver what his parents had done to him. Oliver would never wonder whether his father loved him. For that matter, he would never have to wonder *who* his father was. Once the paternity test was done, Aiden would have that sewn up for them both.

"Turn him around, facing you. So I can rinse out his hair."

He carefully turned Oliver in his hands, but it wasn't easy—it was like holding on to a greased-up watermelon with moving arms and legs. "I'm trying to figure out how I'm supposed to do this by myself."

"I ordered a seat that goes in the tub. That will help immensely. And it won't be long before he can sit up reliably in the bath on his own."

Now that he and Oliver were facing each other, Aiden had a chance to really study him. Oliver returned the gaze, chewing on a rubbery red fish. His eyes were so sweet and innocent, full of wonder. Aiden saw only hope, remarkable considering what the little guy had been through. As Sarah rinsed his hair, Aiden was overcome with the most unusual feeling. It was stronger than his inclination to protect Oliver from big waves. It was a need to keep him from everything bad. He never wanted Oliver's eyes to reflect anything but happiness. Had his own father ever looked at him like this? He didn't enjoy the role of pessimist, but the idea was implausible.

Sarah rolled a small bar of soap in her delicate hands and washed Oliver's back, shoulders and stomach, while Aiden held on tight. Every gentle caress showed someone who genuinely cared about her charge. He'd never really seen this side of any woman aside from on TV or in movies, and it was breathtaking to watch. If he were honest, he'd never done so many things with a woman that gave him a taste of what being a couple was like. Wining, dining and seduction were not the same. This was different.

Sarah swept her hair to one side, displaying the stretch of her graceful neck, the contours of her collarbone. Her skin was so touchable, and the urge to do exactly that was strong with her mere inches away. His hands were practically twitching at the idea. He had to set his mind on another course.

"So. Tell me more about you," he said.

She smiled and sat back on her haunches. "Not much to tell. Born and raised in Ohio, oldest of five. Moved to Boston to study fashion design, stayed for the good nanny jobs."

"Why not go right into design?"

She plucked a washcloth from the bathroom vanity and wiped her hands. "Nannying was a detour. I grew up helping out with my siblings, so it was a natural thing to care for children. And Boston is not cheap. Nannying pays well. It just worked."

"If you liked it that much and it paid well, how does that stop working?"

She looked down at the floor, her golden hair falling down around her face. "I burned out. Badly. Let's put it that way."

That didn't make sense. She didn't seem at all burned out on caring for Oliver. If anything, she had superhuman stamina and patience when it came to it. "And the rest? Surely there's a special guy in your life."

"There is." Her face lit up so brightly that it was as if someone had sucker punched him. So much for seduction. There was another man.

"His name is Oliver," she continued. "He's so sweet. He doesn't talk much. Drools a fair amount. Still learning how to walk. Exactly like I like my men."

He laughed and shook his head. She was ridiculously charming and clever, probably why he had such a strong reaction to the idea of her with a boyfriend.

She flipped her hair back and grinned at Oliver. "But seriously, the right guy hasn't walked into my life and I'm not about to wait. I'm too busy trying to build my business to think about stuff like that. Romance is not on my radar right now."

No wonder he'd been feeling as though he and Sarah might be kindred spirits, even though they came from different worlds. She wasn't looking for love. And neither was he. And with only ten days together, that might be perfect.

Sarah was ready to claim victory over bath time—Oliver was clean and she hadn't been caught staring at Aiden. It was a miracle since she'd been doing exactly that, sneaking peeks at his chest, broad and firm with the most perfect patch of dark hair in the center. Then there were his glorious shoulders and his sculpted biceps. She'd also spent a fair amount of time studying the tattoo on the inside of his forearm—a dark and intriguing pattern, impossible to decipher.

She bopped Oliver on the nose with the tip of her finger. "Hey, mister. It's time for somebody to get out of the bath and get into pj's."

Aiden furrowed his brow. "Sarah's no fun," he said to Oliver. "I don't know about you, but I'm good for at least another fifteen minutes."

She smiled. "The water will be freezing by then. And don't forget the schedule."

"Ah, yes. The schedule."

Aiden lifted Oliver out of the bath and handed him to Sarah, who had a towel at the ready. She wrapped up the baby, holding him close, gently drying his hair with an extra washcloth. Her vision drifted to Aiden as he climbed out and planted one foot on the edge of the tub and bent over to scrub his leg with the towel. She nearly bit right through her lip. His back was long and lean, his posture flaunting the definition—a railroad of muscle running north to that thick, touchable head of hair and south to a pleasingly tight rear view.

He dropped his foot and turned. Either she hadn't had *time* to turn away or she hadn't had the will. A devilish half smile crossed his face—a grin that said he knew she'd just committed his backside to memory. Sarah was petrified. If she shied away, she'd look even more guilty. It'd be tantamount to blurting, *I had to look. You're too hot* not *to look*. But if she kept staring, it would be hard to stop and that would further chip away at her resolve. No falling for the impossibly handsome single dad with the adorable baby.

"You're wet." Aiden nodded in her direction, wrapping the towel around his waist.

Sarah shifted Oliver to her hip. Her dress was streaked with dark patches and clung to her thighs. "Oh, shoot. Yeah. I should probably get out of this thing."

"Might as well get comfortable since we're in for the night."

"Comfortable?" *No, not comfortable. I need to get uncomfortable.*

"Unless an evening gown is more appropriate for story time. I'm still learning here." He took the baby from her. They were ridiculously cute together—Aiden bare chested and wearing a towel, Oliver bundled up in his arms. "If Oliver gets to wear pajamas, that's what I'm wearing, too. You might as well join us."

"I didn't pack for a pajama party. All I have is one of my nightgowns."

"I haven't seen your work yet. If I'm going to help you with your business, I need to know what you're selling."

"I'll show you pictures."

"Why? Too sexy?"

"No," she blurted, not taking the time to think.

"Then what's the problem?" He cast her a look of admonishment that left her quaking. "If this is what you do, you have to own it. You have to live it or it'll never work."

"I do live it. I do own it."

"Then show me. I promise I'll contain myself."

She stifled her exasperation. "Fine. Everything you need to get Oliver dressed is on your bed. I'll be right back."

"Don't take too long. I'm still figuring out this whole diaper thing."

Sarah hustled down the hall in her bare feet, muttering to herself. "Great job, Sarah. First you get caught staring and now he talked you into half-naked story time."

How had she ended up in this situation? *Aiden.* He was everything she hadn't expected. Once she'd gotten past the get-out-of-my-office exterior and been invited into his inner sanctum, he'd shown her a different side, one that was unfairly appealing. He was nicer, he was more amenable, he was generous. And then there were the things his physical presence did to her, making her tingle in places that hadn't tingled in more than a year. Not since she'd discovered that her employer Jason had been taking her to bed when he was in town and doing the same with countless other women when he traveled for work. She'd allowed herself to get caught up in their lives, and crossed the line no nanny should, and she'd paid the price. Her heart had been trampled by Jason, and even worse—she'd had to say goodbye to Chloe, his sweet, adorable daughter. That had hurt like nothing else. She couldn't repeat that mistake.

She ducked into her room and closed the door, sucking in a deep breath to reclaim some semblance of control. She would not be her own worst enemy. Time to get her act together.

Her eyes darted to her suitcase, perched on the bench at the foot of her bed. Unless some different pajamas had magically made their way inside, she had exactly one of her designs with her—a midthigh bias-cut nightgown with thin straps. The black raw silk held a subtle shimmer, embroidered with delicate silver threads at the hem and demure neckline. It didn't scream sexpot, but it wasn't anywhere close to frumpy either. Just risqué enough to give her an anxiety attack. Her shoulders dropped in defeat.

"He said I have to own it. I just have to do that." There was no more time for thinking. Aiden was indeed still figuring out the whole diaper thing, and Oliver would invariably pee all over him if she took too long. She wrestled her way out of her dress and threaded the chemise over her head. The silk skimmed her skin, reminding her precisely why her customers couldn't get enough of her nightgowns—they made a woman feel sexy.

But she could take the edge off. She grabbed her black cardigan and put it on, buttoning it up. She'd bought herself a small measure of modesty, but as she stole a passing glance in the mirror, she saw that she was not owning it—she was borrowing it. Frustration bubbled up inside her, but she couldn't simply traipse into Aiden's bedroom dressed for seduction. This would have to do. If she had to walk a narrow tightrope, she would. Even if she'd be donning a bizarre ensemble while doing it.

With no more time for second-guessing, she hurried back down the hall. Aiden's door was open. He was hunched over the side of the bed, attempting to dress Oliver.

Sarah joined them, perching gingerly on the edge of the mattress. The bedding was so soft and silky she had to stifle a moan of approval. In dark gray pajama pants and a black T-shirt that showed off the straight line of his shoulders, Aiden was dressed to kill. Why did everything about him have to be so enticing? "Looks like you did well with the diaper. What about the rest?"

"I'm worried I'm going to bend him in the wrong direction."

"Just think about how you would get ready for bed. Do that."

He arched an untamed eyebrow at her. "Then he's ready. Because I don't wear much to bed."

Of course he just *had* to plant that mental image in

her head. He had to. "Then pretend you're putting on a shirt for work." She crossed her legs, noticing how parts of her were again tingling and zipping with electricity.

Aiden got Oliver into the sleeves and the legs, but then he hit another trouble spot with the snaps. "These things don't match up."

"Start at the top."

He did as she'd instructed and picked up Oliver when he was done. "Good?"

"Fantastic."

He sat next to her on the bed, Oliver in his lap. "You know, I can hardly see what you're wearing with that big old sweater over the top of it."

She wrapped her arms around her waist. "I was cold," she lied. Being this close to Aiden, she was about to go up in flames. "And we need to get going with bedtime."

"Right. The schedule."

Nightgown crisis averted, it was now acceptable to exhale.

"Since the crib doesn't come until tomorrow, Oliver can sleep with you tonight. It will be a nice way for you two to bond."

"But what if I roll onto him? What if he falls out of the bed?"

A breathy laugh escaped her lips.

"Something funny?" he asked.

"Careful. You sound like a dad."

"They're valid questions."

"And I'm glad you're concerned. We can put some dining chairs next to the side of the bed."

Aiden scratched his head, looking around the room. "Get up. Hold Oliver."

Sarah stood and took the baby, watching as Aiden pushed aside the bench at the foot of his bed and began tugging on his mattress. It only took a few pulls before it landed with a thump on the floor.

"There. Then if he rolls out of bed, he won't go far. It's only for one night."

Sarah could hardly believe her eyes. "Talk about problem solving."

"It's partly selfish. I won't get any sleep if I'm paranoid all night about what's going to happen to him."

She didn't bother containing her smile, even though she sensed that with every sweet thing Aiden did or said, she was being pulled more forcefully into his orbit. "You're turning into a dad right before my eyes."

Aiden retrieved the pillows from their resting place on the box spring—they hadn't made the trip. "I have a job to do, I don't shy away from it."

"I know, but you were bitching about baby gates a few hours ago. Now you're camping out in your own bedroom."

Aiden stepped over to her and took Oliver. "It was the bath. I guess it started to sink in that he needs me. It feels nice. Nobody's ever needed me like he does."

There was an edge of sadness to Aiden's voice that tugged at Sarah's heart. She needed to make a graceful exit, now. "You know, I think I'm going to get Oliver a bottle and walk you through the bedtime routine. Something tells me you'll do just fine."

"Oh, okay. Did you want to have dinner after he goes to sleep?"

I do. I really do. But I don't. "No, thank you. I've had a long day. I'll just turn in."

Aiden seemed puzzled, but didn't argue. "Okay."

Sarah retrieved Oliver's bottle and left Aiden to his own devices after a brief overview of what to do. Since Oliver's nap had been cut short that day, she was sure he'd fall asleep quickly. Apparently, exactly that had happened, since she didn't hear another peep for hours. She stayed in her room, tucked under the covers, trying to banish thoughts of Aiden from her head.

Deep in the middle of the night, Sarah woke to the sound of Oliver's cries. They caused her physical pain, made worse by the fact that she couldn't go to him. Aiden had to learn how to deal with it. The baby let out another screech and Sarah rolled onto her side, squinting at the alarm clock on the bedside table. Two forty-three.

This was normal. No big emergency. Oliver cried again and her instinct told her to go to him, and if she were honest, there was sympathy for Aiden, too. He'd been through a lot today and had risen to the occasion. She sat up, dangling her feet off the edge of the bed, listening. There was quiet. She was just about to lie back down when another cry came.

As did a knock on the door. "Sarah? Are you up?"

Hearing Aiden's voice in the middle of the night did something funny to her. "Yes. Need some help?"

Oliver wailed again.

"Yeah. If that's okay."

"Two secs." Sarah climbed out of bed and opened the door. There stood a nearly naked Aiden, wearing only a pair of gray boxer briefs, and a red-eyed Oliver. The baby lunged for her and Sarah took him, bouncing him in her arms to comfort him. "What's wrong, buddy? Why are we giving Daddy such a hard time on his first night?"

Aiden walked in and sat down on the edge of her bed, running his hands through his hair. "I thought I was in good shape. He started to get fussy and then he started to cry, so I got up and changed his diaper. He was pretty wet."

Sarah nodded, pacing back and forth, partly to comfort Oliver, and partly to distract herself from the vision of Aiden. "Good."

"He didn't want a bottle."

"Did you try his pacifier?"

"I couldn't find that thing. I think it's somewhere in the bed."

"That might help. Let's go look."

She followed Aiden down the hall into his bedroom, where he flipped on one of the bedside lamps. His daddy instincts were already becoming attuned. Most first-time parents would've flipped on the overhead light. She bounced Oliver up and down while Aiden kneeled down on the bed and began rummaging through the sheets.

"Ha. Found it." Aiden stood, victorious, and brought his finding to Oliver. The baby grabbed the pacifier with his hand and plugged it right into his mouth. "So that's what he wanted."

"Apparently."

Aiden blew out a breath. "I have a lot to learn. But thanks for your help." He reached for Oliver, but the baby was having none of that, clinging to Sarah and whimpering. "He wants you. Maybe you should take him for the rest of the night."

"Oh no. You have a way bigger bed than I do. And you two are supposed to be bonding, anyway."

"So sleep in my bed with us. I'm too tired to argue."

"That hardly seems appropriate."

"Why? We're going to have a baby between us. You'll have to trust me when I say that nothing will happen, however tempting you might be, Sarah Daltrey."

Tempting? Yeah, right.

"And there'll be plenty of room. You're practically a miniature human being."

"I'm not miniature."

"Like I said, too tired to argue. Just get in the bed. Please."

"Fine. But tonight only."

"I won't need to have you in my bed tomorrow night. There'll be a crib."

Well, that certainly solved that, didn't it? She walked around to the other side of the bed, and climbed in under the covers. Even with the mattress directly on the floor, she'd never been on a more comfortable bed in her entire life. Oliver must've been really unhappy to have had a hard time sleeping.

Aiden turned out the light and joined them, lying on his side, facing her and Oliver. The baby relaxed and let go of his iron grip on her shoulder, settling in on his back between them. The quiet was thick and nearly unbearable. She was too keenly aware that she was in bed with Aiden and that Aiden was aware of her and that Aiden was still awake. It was going to take forever to fall asleep.

"Sarah," Aiden whispered.

"What?"

"You let me see the nightgown."

Sleep deprivation makes me dumb. "I guess I did."

"It's gorgeous. I'm not surprised you're having a hard time keeping inventory."

She smiled to herself, there in the darkness.

"You were wrong when you said it wasn't sexy."

Sarah's heart galloped at an unhealthy speed. Now she'd really never get to sleep.

"It shows off your legs. You have nice legs," he continued. "And, well, it compliments other parts of you as well."

If it were possible to die from flattery, Sarah was DOA. What was she supposed to say to that? Was she supposed to reciprocate? *Those boxers you're wearing sure show off your three percent body fat and ridiculously alluring physique?*

"Sarah? Are you asleep?"

Dang. She should've pretended to be snoring. "Not quite," she whispered.

"Did I say something wrong?"

No. You said everything right. "I think we should get some sleep. And I don't want to wake the baby."

Six

Aiden was rarely overwhelmed. He didn't believe in it. Why panic when there's a lot to do? Tackle it, and move on. But bleary-eyed, navigating the maze of boxes in the hall outside Oliver's nursery and operating on very little sleep, he was officially off his game.

"How does a person who is so small need so much stuff?"

"You asked me the same thing yesterday. And I don't know why, they just do." Sarah balanced Oliver on her hip while she peeked into his room, where two delivery people were assembling furniture. "They should have the crib done soon. Somebody needs to sleep in his own bed tonight." She cleared her throat and looked square at Aiden. "That goes for me, too."

"Of course." Yeah, he'd gotten the hint last night

when he'd tried to say a few nice things and she'd hardly reacted at all. Although he'd caught her staring when he'd climbed out of the bath, and the look in her eyes said she approved, so which was it? It seemed like she was attracted to him, but maybe not.

It might have been a bad idea to invite Sarah into bed last night, but that was also his first dose of sleep deprivation at the hands of a crying baby. He could already see how a parent could end up giving in to any number of demands, just to have a respite.

Of course he hadn't slept soundly. He'd worried that he might crush little Oliver, so he'd made a point of not moving, which didn't lend itself to relaxation. He'd been intensely aware of every peep the baby made, hoping he'd sleep through the rest of the night. Sarah's presence hadn't helped. He'd ended up in bed with women in fewer than twenty-four hours before, but never like this, and never with a woman like her. As he'd studied her in the soft light that morning, he found himself not only admiring her uncommon beauty—the scattering of faint freckles across her cheeks, and lips that could make him lose all sense of direction if he thought about them too much—he had to extol the gumption contained in her small frame. She'd gotten through to him when that was the last thing he allowed.

"How are we supposed to get all of this put away with a toddler crawling all over the house?" he asked.

"Now you understand the challenge of caring for a child. It's a constant juggling act."

Oliver struggled and kicked to get down from Sarah's hip.

"So I'm learning." He yawned and took another sip of his coffee. This was going to be a long day. Not that he wasn't looking forward to it. As much as he'd never imagined spending his weekend this way, and as tired as he was, yesterday had been incredible.

"He'll go down for his morning nap soon and he'll have the longer one in the afternoon. That should give us some time. Of course, it'd be a lot easier if we brought in reinforcements. Maybe you could call your family?"

Not this again. "I already told you I'm not ready for Oliver to be around my mom at all, let alone have her come in and spend any time with him on her own."

"What about Anna? Didn't she offer to watch him? She could take him for a walk and some fresh air."

That could work. Anna was Aiden's strongest ally in his family. He and his brother Adam had their moments, but he also represented some of the most painful parts of Aiden's childhood—their father pitting the boys against each other, and deeming Adam heir apparent, even when logic said that Aiden, as the oldest child, should've eventually been handed the reins at LangTel.

Aiden's other family ally was Anna's husband, Jacob. He and Aiden were cut from a similar cloth—both dealing with the price a man must pay when he's had a strained relationship with his father.

"Anna would love it."

Sarah let Oliver down onto the floor. With the help of a cardboard box, he pulled himself to standing and began pounding on the top. "Yes. Please call your sister."

Anna and Jacob were over to the apartment in less than an hour. Oliver was still taking his nap when they arrived. Sarah and Anna had gone up to Aiden's room, so Anna could watch Oliver sleep. Talk about baby fever—Anna had it.

"Now that you've had twenty-four hours to come to terms with it, how's fatherhood?" Jacob asked, settling in on the living room couch.

"Surreal. That's the best way to describe it." He scratched his head and glanced out the window—the sky was crystal clear. Not a single cloud. "Honestly, it's the only way to describe it. It doesn't feel real."

"I take it you're going to have a paternity test?"

"We have to for my name to be added to Oliver's birth certificate. Then Sarah will sign over guardianship."

"Is there any chance he might not be yours?"

After his first look into Oliver's eyes yesterday, and especially after seeing his birthmark, Aiden had been viewing the paternity test as nothing more than a formality. There was no way that Sarah could've popped into his life with a baby that looked *just* like him. But the question brought up feelings he'd wrestled with for so long. Had his dad done a paternity test? Was that the moment when things went wrong? When Roger Langford decided he wanted nothing to do with him?

"I don't want to entertain the thought, to be honest. I look in his eyes and I know he's my son. It's the best feeling, even if it has been out of the blue."

Jacob smiled and stretched his arm across the back of the couch. "I can't believe Anna and I are so close. Only six weeks until her due date. Talk about surreal, try touching someone's stomach and feeling a kick and realizing there's a tiny person in there."

"Are your parents excited about becoming grandparents? That's a lot of pressure on you as an only child."

"My mom says she is, but we'll have to wait and see what happens. Your mom, on the other hand. All she talks about is the baby."

That gave Aiden a sliver of optimism.

"Look who's up from his nap." Anna waltzed into the room, talking in a happy singsong, holding Oliver and smiling warmly at him. It was funny the effect that Oliver had on people. Aiden felt as though he'd been given a ray of sunshine.

Jacob got up from the couch and went to Anna, wrapping his arm around her back. "Holding a baby suits you. You look perfect."

Anna's smile only grew. "Oliver is perfect. I have the perfect nephew. It's a fact."

Aiden soaked up the joy radiating from his sister. He needed to share Oliver with his family, which meant he needed to get his mother up to speed and invite her over to meet him. It was time to let her in. Aiden walked over to Anna as Oliver cuddled with her. He pressed a gentle kiss to his petal-soft cheek. *This child will always know love.* Oliver would never doubt that he was wanted and adored. Not for a minute.

"If you guys are going to take him on a walk, I'll show you how to use the stroller."

As she watched the elevator doors to Aiden's apartment draw closed, and Oliver, along with Anna and

Jacob, disappeared from sight, Sarah was struck by one thought. *We're alone.*

She turned and walked square into Aiden's chest.

"Slow down, champ." He grasped her shoulders. "I know they won't be gone long, but we have time to get down to business."

Get down to business. Why did her brain have to translate everything he said into a rambling internal dialogue about *S-E-X*?

"No time like the present." She laughed nervously. He still hadn't let go, and his warmth poured into her like a waterfall into a thimble. She was sure he was trying to hypnotize her with his blue eyes.

A smile rolled across his lips and Sarah was now distracted by his mouth. It was so tempting, so kissable, and she was dying of curiosity. Which version of Aiden Langford would she get if she kissed him? The powerful, broad-shouldered businessman? Walking sex in a suit? He'd probably want to be in charge in the bedroom. Or would it be the effortlessly sexy tattooed guy in board shorts? The one who needed space and jumped out of planes? She could see that guy taking his time, tending to the small touches that send a woman over the edge. She shuddered at the realization—she wanted both.

"I just want to thank you." With no other sound in the apartment, the timbre of his husky voice echoed in her head.

"For what?"

"For bringing Oliver to me. I never imagined I would feel like this."

"That's a big turnaround from the guy who ignored my emails and phone calls for three weeks."

He nodded like a man accepting guilt, a storm of blues and grays swirling in his eyes. "I know. And I apologize. I didn't want to believe it was true. It's impossible to know how you'll feel about parenthood until you have a child. If you'd asked me two days ago if I wanted a baby, I would've said absolutely not. I don't feel like that anymore."

Sarah's ovaries were whispering to her, *God, he's good.* A ridiculously hot guy confessing his tender feelings for a baby? Forget about it. After the bath last night and later being in his bed, Sarah was tempting fate. She needed to keep things professional. "It's been nice to watch you and Oliver connect. That makes me happy. Now let's go upstairs and get his room squared away."

Aiden released her from his grasp, leaving shockwaves of heat. He drew in a deep breath through his nose, studying her face. "Okay. Whatever you say."

Sarah did an abrupt about-face to lead the way upstairs.

"Hold on a sec," Aiden said.

"What?"

"Since when do I have a cookie jar?"

"Since you left me alone with the internet and your credit card. You have a little boy in the house. You need a cookie jar."

"I thought nannies didn't allow children to have things like cookies."

Sarah shrugged. "It's nice to show someone how much you love them by giving them something sweet."

She resumed her trek to the stairs, holding her finger up in the air. "Just not every day."

Upstairs, the dark wood crib was waiting in the corner of Oliver's room. There was a combination dresser and changing table, and a beautiful rocking chair as well. All it needed were finishing touches—artwork, more books, his most precious toys—the special things that would make Oliver feel at home.

Sarah had already washed the crib bedding. "Let's make up his bed. I'll show you how to lower the side of the crib."

Aiden stood by her side, again making her nervous, as she showed him how to lift up on the side rail of the crib before lowering it. "Seems simple enough."

"Be sure that the side always goes up. You don't want him escaping."

"Or staging a coup."

"Very funny. Since Oliver's pulling up on furniture, the mattress is on the lowest setting. It goes at the top for a newborn. To save your back."

"Unless there's something I don't know, I wouldn't ever need to put it up higher, would I?"

Sarah started to put on the waterproof mattress pad and Aiden helped at the other end. "Maybe you'll get married and have another baby." Why she'd chosen to go on a fishing expedition was beyond her.

"I'd have to keep a woman around for more than a few days for that to happen."

Leave it to Aiden to casually own up to his playboy ways. "I take it your very short relationship with Oliver's mom was the norm?" Gail had been spare with her account of Aiden, saying that he was charming and sexy and up-front about not wanting anything serious. Sarah couldn't blame her for a second for going for it. She would've done the same thing if she were brave enough to have a fling. She'd never had a talent for walking away from an amazing guy.

"Remember when I said that I need space? That includes my love life."

"Space. That's such a cop-out." Sarah might have subjected herself to horrible heartbreak, but at least she'd taken chances for love.

"Excuse me?"

"So, you'll jump out of an airplane, but getting serious with someone is off-limits? You meet a woman and you decide before the start that it's going nowhere."

"No, I decide precisely where it's going. I know how it ends. I know my limitations and I accept them."

Sarah draped two small blankets over the end of the crib. "If that's what makes you happy, that's great. I just don't think you're being honest with yourself. You said you need space, but it didn't take long for you to get comfortable with Oliver."

"That's not the same thing, at all. Oliver needs me. And what about you? You're the one who said you won't make time for a boyfriend."

"My situation is completely different."

"How?"

"Because I refuse to treat a man as temporary." *Exactly the way they tend to treat me.* "But you treat women that way. It's sad, really."

"I don't need you to feel sorry for me."

"Oh, I don't. So don't worry about it." She shook her head. She had to escape this line of conversation. She'd learned enough frustrating details for one day. Aiden was everything she'd first thought—the guy who does not commit. "Can we please talk about my business? I need you to hold up your end of the deal. I'm at the point where Kama could either take off or crash and burn."

"Kama? Is that what it's called?"

"Yes. It's the Hindu god of desire. Our fabrics all come from India, so I thought it was fitting."

He nodded and jutted out his lower lip. "I like it. Simple. Elegant. Plus, it makes me think of the *Kama Sutra* and you know what that makes me think of."

You walked right into that one. "Will you please take this seriously? The next six months are crucial and I don't know what I'm supposed to do. I'm terrified it will fail." That was an understatement. She couldn't imagine a future without Kama. She'd be left to start all over again, doing what, she had no idea.

"It really is important to you, isn't it? Your little business of making nightgowns."

"Don't be so dismissive. It's my livelihood. My career."

"And like I said last night, if it means that much to you you have to own it. You were hiding it from me last night. That's troublesome."

I was hiding me from you last night. Not the same thing.

"And whatever you say, you still have nannying," he continued. "There will always be children to care for and you're so good at it. Not everyone is an entrepreneur."

"I don't know how many times I need to tell you. I am *not* a nanny."

"Now who's living a contradictory life? I watch you with Oliver and you clearly adore him. So you love kids, but refuse to earn a living that way?"

"I want the challenge of making this work."

"That's it?"

"That's it." *That's all I'm going to tell you.*

"Okay, then. Walk me through the whole thing."

"Let me show you." She pulled up some photos on her phone. She'd taken them to show the bank when things started to take off and she'd tried to get a loan for expansion. "Flip through these. You'll see some of what I'm up against."

He swiped at the screen. "It's tiny. How can you get anything done in this space?"

"Honestly? I have no idea, other than I have some incredible employees who are willing to put up with a lot. I have six people doing assembly. If I were going to keep up with demand, I could easily have two dozen, but I'd have nowhere to put them. Moving means a huge lease, more equipment, health insurance and finding qualified people. It's a lot. I barely sleep as it is."

"So outsource. Let someone else do your manufacturing."

"I can't fire these people. They've been with me since the beginning, and they all do exceptional work. They have families to support."

"You're destroying your margins."

"Not if I'm in with the right retailers and can demand a better price point. Plus, our margins will improve once we've streamlined our manufacturing."

"Okay, then. Why don't I become an investor? I'll write a check and we can be done."

Here was Aiden's propensity for clean and simple, in sharp focus. It wasn't merely his attitude toward romance—he did this with everything that could get messy. No matter what, he was *not* going to become her investor. She needed to see out this ten days and get out of Dodge before his eyes made her do something she would regret.

"I need guidance. I need someone to give me advice and help me make the right connections, not throw money at me and hope I'll go away. That's your role in our arrangement and now you're trying to get out of it." She didn't want to speak to him in this manner, but she hated being blown off. It felt too much like Jason discounting everything about her—her dreams, her desires, and most important, the feelings she'd thought were between them, the ones he'd said were a figment of her overactive imagination.

Aiden handed her back her phone, appraising her. It was as if she could see the gears turning in his head, and she was more than a little nervous to hear what he was going to say. "You're right. I said I'd help you and I will. Not having looked at your financials, I'm thinking we need to find you an exclusive partnership. Become a subsidiary of a larger fashion corporation to scale your production, help with facility and warehousing issues, and most importantly, take over distribution so you can focus on what you're good at."

Finally, he got what she wanted. And he wasn't trying to back out. "Yes. Great. I can spend my time designing." *And I can be back on track.*

Seven

Sunday had brought Aiden's less sunny side. He'd finally called his mother about Oliver that morning, which had not gone as he'd hoped. He'd assumed, and so had Sarah, that she would be eager to come over right away. Instead, she'd said she was busy and would stop by Monday. That response had prompted Aiden to hunker down in his home gym for hours, lifting weights and running on the treadmill. As if the man needed to be in better shape.

Sarah had tried her best to go about her day, working on Oliver's room while he played, and during his nap, doing research on apparel companies she could partner with, per Aiden's suggestion. She'd also taken Oliver for a long walk, with a stop at a bookstore for some of her favorite children's reads. Considering how much

Aiden loved books, she knew the gesture would be appreciated. Maybe someday those books would make him think of her—the woman who'd brought him Oliver out of the blue. And slipped away just as fast.

Now that it was late Monday morning, Sarah was still awaiting the return of pleasant Aiden. He'd been a real jerk during the nanny interviews, which was not the way it should've gone. The agency was the top in the city. Money was no object. All signs led to this being a short and simple process. But she hadn't counted on Aiden stonewalling.

"What is your problem?" Sarah asked as the elevator doors closed on the fourth and final candidate. "For now, the agency has no more nannies to send. The woman was practically Mary Poppins and you tell her that you don't think she's right for Oliver?"

Aiden shoved his hands into the pockets of his dark gray suit pants. He'd ditched the jacket and tie for the interview, but otherwise dressed handsomely, which was driving Sarah crazy. It took too much work to be mad at him when he looked so good.

"Did you see her face when she wasn't talking? It was so cold and stern. I want Oliver to be happy, not scared out of his mind."

"Are you saying she had resting bitch face? Is that really what this has come down to? Because you're being ridiculous."

"I didn't like her. End of story."

Sarah grumbled. Aiden might be right about the woman's austere facial expressions, but she was otherwise perfect. Plus, she was in her fifties and happily married and there was a very petty part of Sarah that wasn't about to leave Aiden with a perky twenty-something.

She flipped through the candidates' résumés. "What about Frances? She had a very sunny personality and came with impeccable references. She was a nanny for Senator Meyers, for God's sake. Do you think just anyone gets that job?"

"And why doesn't she have that job anymore? I'm not sure I buy her answer."

"She wanted to be in New York to help with her sick aunt. The Senator and his family are in Washington, DC. Seems reasonable to me."

"What if her aunt's illness takes over her life? I need someone who is solely focused on Oliver. That's what's best for him."

"You've spent all of three days with him. How can you say that you know what's best?"

Aiden shot her a look that said she'd taken it too far. He swallowed so hard that his Adam's apple bobbed. "I'm trusting my gut. That's the best thing I have to go on right now." He turned and walked out of the entryway and into the kitchen.

Sarah followed. They had to get the nanny situation resolved. "Don't forget that I'm the expert on this subject. I'm telling you right now that you're an idiot of the highest order for sending those four women away."

"We have to keep looking."

"I'm only here for a week, Aiden. It's Monday. Your ten days are up on Sunday and I'm gone. What are you going to do then?"

He grabbed an apple out of the bamboo bowl on the kitchen island. "Maybe I need you to stay longer."

So that's what he was doing—avoiding the potential mess of someone who might not be right by trying to keep the one thing he knew would work—her. "You're trying to force me to stay by sending away the other nannies?"

"Listen to what you just said. *Other* nannies."

"No way. I'm done with that."

"Honestly, I don't believe you're capable of walking away from Oliver on Sunday. You love him. I can see it."

Why did he have to make this so much worse? His words cut to her core. They were the truth and he knew it. "Of course I love Oliver. How could I not? But he's not my child and just like every other child I've cared for, I eventually have to leave him." Just saying the words brought up an unholy mess of things she dreaded and terrible memories. If she was bad at anything, it was goodbye.

"So you've got leaving down to a science. You can do it. No problem." Everything in his tone was biting, dripping with sarcasm.

"I'm not heartless."

"Which is why I don't buy it."

"Look. You need to focus on holding up your end of our deal. Part of that is hiring a nanny. I'm calling the agency to see if they have anyone else for us to interview." She slapped the résumés down on the kitchen counter. "In the meantime, I'd appreciate it if you would please look these over again and see if you're willing to reconsider any of these applicants." She turned on her heel and took extralong strides to get to the stairs.

"Sarah. Hold on."

She turned back, just in time to see him push aside the résumés. "What?"

He blew out a breath. "I'm sorry. I'm sorry if it seems like I have ridiculous standards, but my gut is telling me that those women were not right. Remember, this is all new to me. Almost too new. I'm doing my best. I swear."

She crossed her arms, hoping it would make it easier to buffer her attraction to him. It was hopeless when he was being sweet about the baby and talking in that tone that made her want to flatten him against the wall and climb him like a tree. "I know you're trying. I'm just antsy about time. We don't have much and I have to get back to Boston and Kama."

"I know you do, which is the other thing I need to say to you. Anna and I are working on getting us into a charity fashion show, organized by *Fad Forward Magazine*. Apparently it's a big deal."

Holy crap. Sarah clamped her hand over her mouth to keep a string of elated profanity from leaving her lips. "The Forward Style show? Where is it this year?"

"Miami. I thought I'd just buy tickets, but you have to be invited, which seems ludicrous since it's a charity event..."

Sarah couldn't breathe. She'd seen the pictures in *Fad Forward Magazine* every year since she was a teenager. Their annual charity fashion show was a chance for designers to bring out their most adventuresome work, and was attended by fashion legends, rock stars, Hollywood bigwigs and sometimes even royalty.

"Everybody who's anybody will be there. But I'm not sure it will help me."

"Our target is Sylvia Hodge. She's the honorary host this year. Anna and I dug up some info that she's acquiring new brands, but she's about to spend six months in Europe and Asia, looking for designers. If we want to meet face-to-face with her, going to Miami is the only way. And we might have to just walk up to her and start talking. I can't get her to take my call."

"But you're Aiden Langford. Isn't your last name enough?"

"Sylvia Hodge's admin didn't seem to care who I was."

"If we go, what are our chances?"

He shrugged. "No idea. Right now I'm waiting to see if they'll let me buy tickets."

"But the tickets. I can't afford that. They're tens of thousands of dollars."

"It's my treat."

"But it goes so far beyond our agreement."

"You brought me Oliver. It's the least I can do."

After having been away from LangTel for much of Friday and all of Monday so far, Aiden had a mountain of work, but he couldn't focus, not even with the relative quiet of working from home. The clock on the wall was taunting him. Three forty-five. Fifteen minutes until his mother was set to arrive to meet Oliver.

Sarah poked her head into his office, Oliver on her

hip. The baby smiled at him, sweetly tilting his head to the side. This child would be the death of him, in a good way.

"If you're still working, I can hang out with Oliver until your mom arrives," she said. "Then I'll clear out so you three can have some time alone."

Aiden was trying to be optimistic, clinging to the idea that Oliver would bridge the chasm between him and his mother, but he had too many reasons to believe that would not be the case. "Where are you headed?"

"Out for a run. With all of the excitement of waiting to hear about Miami, I'm way too tense. Plus, I haven't worked out in days. I feel like a slob."

His vision drifted over her. She was wearing black leggings that showed off her fit and healthy curves, with a formfitting top that left her bare shoulders on display. Her hair was back in a high ponytail. He stepped out from behind his desk and took Oliver, unable to keep from admiring her. He wrestled with a deep desire to thread his hands into the back of her golden blond hair and pull out the rubber band, tilt her head back and give her the sort of kiss that makes a woman linger for a moment afterward with her eyes half-open.

"You are not a slob. You look incredible."

"You're just saying that because you feel bad about the nanny interviews."

"I'm saying it because you're a beautiful woman and I'd be an idiot if I didn't at least say it out loud."

A wash of pink crossed her cheeks and she fought a smile. If only she knew that it made him that much more attracted to her. If only she knew that she was making every inch of his body draw tight and burn hot.

"Thank you. I appreciate the compliment." She pressed her lips together and gazed up at him. "If you're going to take Oliver, I'll just head out. I should be done in about an hour. I don't know how long your mom is planning on staying, but I can grab a cup of coffee if you want more time."

The gears in Aiden's head whirred. He'd first thought it would be better if he and his mom were alone with Oliver. Keep things simple. But the truth was that he couldn't imagine Sarah not being there. It didn't make any sense, although he wanted to know why. Then he realized that no matter the situation, Sarah calmed him. She took the edge off. She made him believe things would work out. Aside from his sister, he didn't have anyone in his life who did that, but this was different. Sarah wasn't obligated to make him feel good.

"What if I said I wanted you to stay?"

She scrunched up her adorable nose. "What? Really?"

"I could use the moral support. I could use someone on my side. Things with my mother are not easy. I think you've gathered that much by now."

"I have, although you haven't told me the reason why."

Because I don't want to talk about it. "It's complicated. If you're here, it'll keep the conversation light and fun. I could use that right now."

She looked down at herself. "Oh God. I look terrible. I should go change. I don't want her to see me like this."

Before he could think about what he was doing, his fingers cupped her chin. He shouldn't have crossed that line, but he couldn't help himself. "I think you look perfect. Don't change."

She didn't move. He didn't either. Neither of them said a thing, but their eyes connected, as if they were each digging deeper, wanting more.

Sarah broke the spell with a shake of her head. "You're sweet, but there's no way I'm wearing this to meet your mom. And I have no makeup on." She turned and headed out of his office. "Back in five minutes."

Aiden watched her jog away, her leggings accentuating every move. A ripple of steamy thoughts ran through his head—everything he wanted to do with her. It had been a long time since he'd wanted a woman as badly as he wanted Sarah. The question was whether the opportunity would present itself. So far, there was always something in the way.

Aiden wandered into the kitchen, where his housekeeper had put on a pot of coffee. She'd also stocked Sarah's cookie jar with an assortment of biscotti, some of it plain. Oliver regularly chowed down on teething biscuits, and Aiden decided that this was basically the same thing.

"Do you want a cookie?" He offered it to Oliver.

The baby snatched it from his hand and it went right into his mouth, like most things. His eyes grew wide once he'd gotten a taste. Aiden leaned against the counter, enjoying the moment. Sarah was going to leave behind a lot more than a cookie jar on Sunday.

"Good, huh? Just wait until you get older and I can

take you out for hot fudge sundaes or we can get a hot dog at a baseball game." The thought brought with it a peculiar mix of hope and melancholy. Dads did those things with their children. Aiden very much looked forward to having those experiences with Oliver, but they were things he'd missed out on entirely.

Sarah hurried down the stairs. "This is as good as it's going to get. I really wish you would've given me some advance notice. I could've taken a shower and done something with my hair." Her face was flush with color, probably from rushing around. She wore a full black skirt that skimmed her knees and a white top that hinted at the curves he'd been admiring for days now. She'd put on the sandals she'd been wearing the day he met her, which gave her a few more inches of height. He still towered over her, but he loved the way they made her legs look.

"Once again, you look perfect."

The buzzer for the elevator rang.

"You're sweet. And you need to answer the door."

Aiden's heart went from racing over Sarah to plummeting to his stomach. His mother had arrived. He didn't bother with the intercom, hitting the button to grant her access to his floor. "Here goes nothing," he said to Sarah. He filed into the entryway, Oliver in tow and making excellent progress on his cookie.

When the doors slid open, Aiden managed a smile. It was only half-forced. He still loved his mother, despite his immense frustrations with her.

She actually gasped when she saw Oliver, breezing off the elevator in her usual garb of all black with a colorful scarf tied at her neck. She took a direct route to her grandson, her mouth softening to a tiny O. "Aiden, he looks just like you." She held on to his hand and shook her head in disbelief, but not enough to muss her short, dark hair. "What an angel." A tear rolled down her cheek, but then a steady stream started. Of the many reactions he'd anticipated from his mother, full-on crying was not one of them. She smiled through the tears, her eyes crinkling at the corners. "Can I hold him?"

Aiden was stricken with conflicting emotions, ones that didn't belong in one person's head at the same time. He wanted to protect Oliver. But at the same time, there was a yearning—so deep he could feel it—for his mother to accept and love Oliver. He had to take this leap, however much she could end up hurting either of them. "Yes. Of course."

He handed over Oliver, who seemed perplexed. She bounced him up and down as she plopped her handbag on the entry table.

"Come in, Mom. I want you to meet Sarah."

Sarah was pouring herself a glass of water. "Mrs. Langford. It's so nice to meet you. I've…" She paused and looked right at Aiden. "I've heard so much about you."

"Please, call me Evelyn. And I wish I could say the same about you. My son has been remarkably quiet about everything." She turned and shot Aiden a disappointed look, a wordless reprimand. Did she have any idea how hard he was working to keep up his hopes? Intentional or not, she expertly knocked them back down. "Not that I'm surprised. He keeps things to himself. Always."

Eight

Stress radiated off Aiden like August heat off a tin roof—jaw tense, shoulders rigid. Was he always this away around his mother? He must be, because she didn't seem to notice. She was too preoccupied with Oliver, sitting on the floor in the library, offering him toys from a bag Sarah had given her.

"He's smart. I can tell," she said to no one in particular.

Aiden stood sentry, arms crossed squarely at his chest. This was not a bonding moment for him. He was observing, like a hawk.

Sarah walked up behind him and placed her hand on his shoulder. He flinched, then relaxed under her touch. She might have underestimated this burden, and her heart ached because of it. Whatever there was between him and his mother, it was not good. Sarah desperately wanted to know more. Even if it was painful, she wanted to know.

"Is there anything I can get for you?" she whispered to Aiden.

He looked over his shoulder, lowering his face closer to hers. A waft of his heavenly scent hit her nose—warm and masculine, like the sheets on his bed, just like his entire bedroom. "Now who's the sweet one?" he muttered.

You are. When you want to be. "I'm sensing you could use a drink."

"It's only a little past four."

"It's five o'clock in Nova Scotia. I've heard it's lovely there this time of year. Bourbon?"

"On the rocks." He cracked a smile and his shoulders visibly relaxed. She fought the urge to dig her fingers into them, help him unwind while she committed the contours of his broad frame to memory.

"Cocktail, Evelyn?" Sarah asked.

She shook her head and started peekaboo with Oliver. "I'm too in love with my grandson for a drink. But I'll take a diet soda."

"Got it." Sarah went to work, getting Aiden his drink first. He was in greater need. "Here you go." Their fingers brushed when she gave him his glass, sending a tingly recognition through her.

"Thank you. For everything." His voice was low and soft, just as luxurious as the bourbon in the glass. Why did the man she was supposed to stay away from have to be so undeniably sexy?

The elevator rang again.

"That's odd," Aiden said. "I don't know who could be here."

"I'll get it." Sarah hurried to the entryway and buzzed the intercom. "Hello?"

"It's Liam Hanson for Mr. Langford. I'm one of the admins at Barkforth and Sloan."

The paternity test. "I thought you were coming tomorrow morning." Surely this was not the sort of commotion Aiden wanted while his mother was there.

"They asked me to come this afternoon since you need this done right away. They should've called you."

"Come on up."

Aiden joined her. "Great. With my mom here." He must have overheard. He raked his hand through his hair, again showing her the strain she hated seeing on any face, especially on one as handsome as his.

The elevator doors slid open. "Mr. Langford. I'm so sorry if there was a miscommunication. I promise this will be quick. Five minutes and I'm out of your hair."

Aiden nodded. "No, it's fine. We have to get it done. What do you need?"

"It's a cheek swab from you and one from the baby. That's it."

"He's in the other room."

Sarah followed Liam and Aiden into the library.

"Mom, I need Oliver for a minute. The lawyer's office needs to do the cheek swabs for the paternity test so we can take care of the legal end of things."

Evelyn picked up the baby, handing him to Aiden.

"This seems silly. One look at him and it's obvious he's your son."

Aiden snatched Oliver away, much as he had the day Sarah had mentioned the idea of Evelyn caring for him. "It's important for Oliver and me, too. That we know he's my son, for sure."

She took a sip of her soda. "Of course."

Liam took out two plastic tubes and asked Aiden to open his mouth. He swabbed the inside of his cheek, then did the same to Oliver. "All done. We'll have this expedited. I understand the paperwork needs to be taken care of this week."

Aiden nodded. "Yes."

"If it takes until next week, I could always come back down from Boston, I suppose." Had she just said that? She should *not* be straying from the timeline she'd established. With every passing day, they were more comfortable with each other, she more attracted to him, her resolve becoming flimsy. There were signs he might be feeling the same way—the moment when he'd slid his fingers under her chin? The comments about how good she looked?

"It's best if we wrap this up quickly," Aiden said. "Sarah needs to leave on Sunday and return to her business. Oliver and I need to start our life together, too."

Why was her body filled with such utter disappointment at his words? This was what she'd wanted, and it was no time to switch her priorities. *Stay with the plan, Sarah.* "Aiden's right. I really can't be running back to New York."

"Certainly." Liam packed up everything in a messenger bag, which he slung across his chest. "We'll take care of it, Mr. Langford. We should have the results by Friday."

Aiden walked Liam to the elevator and returned with Oliver. There was a shift in the mood, one impossible to ignore. Aiden had said he wanted to keep things short with his mother for this first visit. Evelyn showed no sign of leaving.

"Can I hold him again?" she asked, getting up from the sofa.

Aiden took in a deep breath. "For a few minutes, then Sarah and I have some things to do. Oliver needs a bath and quiet time before bed."

Even if it might have been an excuse, Aiden was clinging to the schedule, and it was adorable. He sat on the couch next to his mother and tried to hand over the baby, but Oliver wanted to stay with Daddy.

"Don't you want to spend time with Grandma?" Evelyn leaned into Aiden, trying to catch Oliver's attention.

"He's still getting used to you, Mom. It might take time."

"Maybe he's unhappy after having that strange man put a stick in his mouth. The whole thing really is silly. He looks just like you."

"We have to follow the proper channels. It's important." Aiden held Oliver close. "He lost his mother a month ago, and that will be something he'll always wonder about. A child needs to know where he came from. He needs to know where he belongs." Aiden's voice cracked, which Sarah had never heard before, not even in the tender moments with Oliver.

"I wasn't trying to upset you."

Aiden cleared his throat. "Mom. Listen to yourself. There's this dark cloud hanging over us and Oliver has given us the perfect chance to talk about it, but you won't let yourself go there, will you? You'd rather keep your secret."

"I have no earthly idea what you're talking about."

"Yes, you do. I've brought this up with you at least three times since I've been back in New York. It's the reason I've been unhappy for most of my life. It's the reason I tried to take over LangTel. And you're sitting here, talking about the paternity of my son like this hasn't been a question in your own life. It's so frustrating I want to scream." His voice didn't waver in the slightest now. It was sheer determination.

Oliver whimpered.

"You've upset the baby," she said.

Oh no.

Aiden pulled Oliver closer and rubbed his back, pecking him on the forehead. "I think you need to leave. I'm not going to pretend that my entire existence in this family hasn't been built on a lie and you won't own up to it. I know that your husband was not my father. I know it with every fiber of my being. And we all act as if that isn't the case."

Sarah gasped. She didn't mean to, but how could she *not*? Roger Langford wasn't Aiden's father? How could that be?

Evelyn reached out and set her hand on Aiden's forearm. "Aiden, darling. Haven't we all been through enough with losing your father? Don't tear us apart even more. I love you and you're my son. That's all that matters."

Sarah turned to sneak upstairs. She had no business being in the room for this.

"No, Sarah. Don't leave," Aiden said.

Did the man have eyes in the back of his head? Sarah looked down at her feet. Damn noisy shoes.

"So that's your response," he said to his mother. "And when you say we lost my father, do you mean my actual father, or Roger? Because I know they're not the same. There's no other explanation for you sending me off to boarding school. There's no other reason why Adam would be deemed heir apparent when I'm the oldest."

"Aiden, there's no good in dredging up the past. And I really don't think we should discuss this in front of a stranger."

"A stranger? You're calling Sarah a stranger? She's nothing of the sort." Aiden bolted from his seat. "It's time for you to go now. You can come back when you're ready to talk. Until then, I don't want to see you."

"You're going to keep me from my grandson?"

"That's all on you. I have nothing to do with it."

Evelyn blew out a breath, just as determined as Aiden. Family gatherings must be a real barrel of laughs with the Langfords. "You'll change your mind. A baby needs his grandmother." She leaned forward and kissed Oliver's forehead, but Aiden kept both arms firmly around him. "Bye-bye, sweet boy. Grandma will see you soon."

With that, Evelyn Langford traipsed out of the room. Aiden stood, facing the entryway, his back to Sarah. All Sarah could hear was her own pulse thumping in her ears. What she was supposed to say? What was she supposed to do? There was no mistaking the pain in his voice. True or not, he believed that he'd been lied to about his father.

"I'm sorry you had to see that," he said. "I'm sure that's the last thing you would've wanted to trade your run for."

She went to him, her heart heavy. "No, Aiden. I'm glad I was here. I mean, if that's what you wanted."

"It *is* what I wanted. Honestly, your presence probably prevented a bigger blowup. One that's been coming for thirty years."

She reached for his arm, wanting to comfort him even more than that. Here she was, stepping into emotional quicksand, the very last place she belonged if she was going to leave on Sunday with her heart in one piece. "I don't believe that you would've blown up in front of Oliver. I really don't."

Aiden managed a smile, but it was as if it had been broken and cobbled back together. There was some part of him inside that was fractured. She'd sensed that about him the day they met, but now she was beginning to understand what had caused it. Her own family was so important to her. They were always there for her. Always. She couldn't imagine growing up the way Aiden had. He might have had money and privilege, but that didn't replace love. That didn't replace knowing where you came from.

"Thank you for being here. That's really all I can say." He tugged her into an embrace with one arm while he held on to Oliver with the other.

She sank against his chest, so drawn to him, every inch of her wanting to make things better. Each second in his arms was another step into his world, but she would've needed a heart of stone to walk away. He needed her. And in that moment, him needing her was everything.

Oliver was sound asleep in his crib, but Aiden stayed, studying the steady rise and fall of his chest as he slept like a starfish—arms above his head, legs splayed, tiny rosebud mouth open. After the upset of his mother's visit, Oliver filled Aiden with contentment he'd never known. If he never had anything more in his life than Oliver, even if he never got the truth from his mother, he could be happy.

He flipped the baby monitor on, then crept out of the room, quietly closing the door. A few steps down the hall, a heavenly smell hit his nose. Sarah was cooking dinner and judging by that one whiff, it was going to be delicious. She was his savior today, but not because she was preparing a meal. She'd been there for him when his composure crumbled and anger threatened to consume him. She'd been his rock.

That left him in a peculiar spot. If he were smart, he needed to work very hard to keep Sarah as a friend, and as part of Oliver's life. He couldn't imagine her not being involved, even if it was only an occasional phone call or a visit on Oliver's birthday. Considering his zero percent success rate with keeping a woman around for more than a few days, logic said he shouldn't allow them to be anything more than friends. He shouldn't cross that line, however attracted he was to her, even when every inch of him wanted her. Between her beauty, her spark and the sweet things she did for him, he didn't see how he was supposed to stay away. He only knew he had to. Giving in to the temptation of Sarah—sweeping her up in his arms and finally tasting her lips, would likely end with her never speaking to him again. For the first time in his life, he didn't want that.

"Whatever you're cooking, sign me up." He strolled into the kitchen.

She had two glasses of red wine waiting. Was she the perfect woman? She was reading his mind. He wanted nothing more than to relax and put his afternoon behind him.

"Good. Because otherwise, it's toast or a protein bar." Her back was to him, and she was humming—something he'd noticed she did every time she was busy in the kitchen. He forced himself still, to keep from walking up behind her, wrapping his arms around her waist, leaning down and kissing the graceful slope of her neck. He wanted to bury his face in her hair, inhale her sweet scent, get lost in her.

But he had to be good. So he slugged back some wine. "What are we having?"

She turned and smiled sweetly. "Pasta. Almost ready."

"Perfect. Thanks for opening a bottle of wine. If you hadn't, I would have." What was he doing? He'd been reprimanding himself moments ago about how Sarah had to stay a friend, and yet he couldn't stop from talking as if he was in pursuit.

She dished the pasta into two bowls. "Sorry it's not fancy."

"If you want fancy, we could take this bottle of wine up to the rooftop when we're done eating. It's a beautiful night." Was this a good idea? No. Did it sound like fun? Yes. "We'll need to bring the baby monitor."

"Okay, Dad." She elbowed him in the ribs and flashed a flirtatious smile. That was it. She was going to kill him before the night was over.

They ate at the kitchen island, chatting about Oliver, squabbling about nanny candidates and whether or not there would be any more people to interview. It wasn't long before dinner was done, the dishes were in the dishwasher and Sarah suggested they open a second bottle of wine.

"The terrace?" *Stop encouraging this.*

"I should grab a cardigan first. In case I get cold."

I can keep you warm. He pressed his lips together to keep the words from escaping. "Okay."

He waited for Sarah outside her room, then led her to the second-floor stairs at the back of the house that took them up to the empty third floor and finally up to the terrace.

The darkening night sky was streaked with purple and midnight blue, the city lights casting a glow across Sarah's face. She rushed across the stone pavers, like a little kid who couldn't contain her excitement. "It's so beautiful up here. Like your own private park." Holding out her arms, she turned enough to make her dress swirl around her legs.

"It's nice, isn't it?" He smiled, admired her, wishing

he could make everything in the world conform to his will—why couldn't he have a free pass for a night, kiss her and have everything return to normal tomorrow?

"After meeting your mom, I think I understand why you need space."

"Very perceptive. Although the physical space is nice for anyone, especially in the city."

He led her to an outdoor sectional couch and lit a kerosene heater. She plopped down, tucking her leg underneath herself. He set the wine bottle on a low table and joined her, keeping his distance, staying in check.

"Do you want to talk about today?" she asked. "Maybe you'll feel better about everything if you just get it out."

He wasn't much of a talker, especially when it came to things like this, but Sarah wasn't like anyone he'd ever considered confiding in. She had no agenda, nothing to gain. And she had to be wondering what was going on. "I've suspected since I was eight that the man I called Dad wasn't my biological father."

Sarah pressed her lips into a thin line. "That's what I thought. I didn't want to eavesdrop on what you were saying to your mom, but it was hard not to hear."

"I'm glad you were there. It made it far less uncomfortable."

"It seemed pretty uncomfortable."

He had to laugh. She didn't shy away from the truth. "Honestly, that was nothing."

"How does an eight-year-old arrive at that conclusion?"

"I was home from boarding school for Christmas break and I overheard them arguing about it."

"Did you ever ask them about it?"

He took a sip of his wine, fighting back memories of standing in the hall of the Langford family penthouse apartment, late at night. He'd been unable to sleep and wanted to ask his mom for a warm glass of milk, but he'd instead heard her say something terrible. *If I could take it back, I would. But I can't change the fact that he's not your child.* "I never said anything to anyone until I was much older. You have to understand, Roger Langford was an imposing man. And he was never very warm to me. He was to Adam and Anna, but not to me. I didn't want to give him another reason to push me out of the family."

"Push you out?"

"They sent me to boarding school after Adam was born. I was seven. I didn't understand why, but they said it was for my own good. Now I suspect it was because he couldn't stand the sight of me."

Sarah's eyes became impossibly sad. He hated seeing that look on her face, even when it was *his* pain she was reflecting. She grasped his forearm, scooting closer on the couch. The distance he'd left was gone, and he was so glad. He craved having her close. He wanted nothing more than to erase the space between them.

"I can't even imagine what that must've been like. I'm sure you were just the sweetest boy. I'm so sorry."

Aiden wasn't much for pity, but it was healing to have Sarah see how wrong it all was. "It got worse over the years. I got in trouble at school a lot, mostly for fighting or practical jokes. I got kicked out of a few. That was never fun. It embarrassed my dad and confirmed to him that I didn't belong at home. I guess I was self-destructive, but I was confused. I certainly didn't feel loved."

Sarah was now rubbing his arm softly with her thumb. "Of course you didn't. No child should feel that way." She looked down at her lap and fiddled with the hem of her sweater. She was so gorgeous in the moonlight—it was like watching a museum masterpiece come to life. "I know that my arrival with Oliver was a shock, but you have such a big opportunity with him."

"Opportunity?"

She nodded and sucked in her lower lip. "You can give Oliver the childhood that you didn't have."

For a moment, it felt as though the earth didn't move. He'd thought that on some level, but hearing her say it made it clear how right it was. "I can break the cycle."

"Yes. Although I don't think you'll have real closure until your mom finally tells you the truth."

He downed the last of his wine. "I'm starting to wonder if that will happen."

"Have you told anyone else in your family?"

"I confided in Anna, but she thinks I'm crazy. She knows that something wasn't right in our household, but I don't think she wants to believe it. My father has only been gone about a year. Everyone is still grieving. No one wants to think ill of him."

"I don't think you're crazy, Aiden. It makes perfect sense to me."

Sarah's lips were right there, waiting for him, telling him everything he'd ever wanted to hear. The validation of his pain, his fears, the vulnerability that he wished didn't exist at all, was so powerful it made his entire body feel lighter. He wanted to kiss her so badly, to express his gratitude for her in a way that would leave no doubt in her mind that he appreciated her.

But he couldn't do that. Not when he needed her in Oliver's life. Not when he was sure it would ruin everything.

His phone buzzed with a text. Normally, he wouldn't stop to read it, especially when he was alone with a beautiful woman, but it was taking extreme effort to keep from kissing this one and it was his intention to do exactly that. "I'm sorry. I should check this." The message was from Anna—good news. "You and I are going to Miami. We have our tickets."

Sarah popped up out of her seat. "For Forward Style?"

He laughed, watching her bounce on her toes. "Yes. We go the day after tomorrow."

"Wednesday? Oh my God. We have to book flights. Who's going to take care of Oliver?" She looked him squarely in the face. "What am I going to wear?"

"We'll ask Anna and Jacob to stay with Oliver for the night. You know they'd love to do it."

Sarah's shoulders dropped with relief. "True. She and Jacob are so good with him. What about the rest?"

"We'll take the corporate jet. No need to worry about flights."

"Are you sure? That seems extravagant."

He grinned so wide it made his cheeks ache. The joy of seeing her happy and excited was his reward after a roller coaster of a day. "Yes. I'm sure. I told you I'd help you, and I'm a man of my word. As for what you should wear, we're in New York. Go shopping."

She shook her head. "There's no time. We have more nannies to interview tomorrow, and I know you need to get some work done. Plus, if I'm going to walk up to Sylvia Hodge and try to impress her, I need to be wearing one of my own designs."

"You're going to wear a nightgown?"

She slapped his arm and grimaced. "No, silly. I design other things. And I have the perfect gown at home. It's gorgeous. Emerald green, dangerously low-cut. Sylvia will love it." Her eyes flashed with mischief. "I just need to get Tessa in my office to overnight it to me."

Aiden felt like he couldn't breathe. In a little more than twenty-four hours, he'd be alone in Miami with Sarah and her dangerous dress. How he loved peril, especially at the hand of a beautiful woman. "Have her send you a swimsuit, too. We can't go to Florida without some fun in the sun."

Nine

Between leaving Oliver overnight, and knowing that
in twelve hours she'd have to dazzle Sylvia Hodge at a
fashion event most people would kill to attend, Sarah
was so worked up she thought she might be sick. "I
hope I haven't forgotten anything." Yesterday had been
such a whirlwind, it'd be a modern miracle if she hadn't
messed up something. Oliver'd had a fussy day, which
probably meant he had another tooth coming in. Aiden
had been shuttered in his home office for hours, coming out long enough to say no to three more nanny
candidates.

Sarah had dealt with a million other details beyond
that, including having Tessa, her assistant, overnight
her gown and a few more clothes to the hotel in Miami.
That meant she was in the same black sundress she'd

had on the day she met Aiden. She didn't feel confident at all, but she'd only packed a weekend's worth of clothes when she'd come to New York. Two days had always been her plan.

"If we have any questions, we'll call you." Anna eased herself into a chair at the kitchen table. "I just want you to go to Miami and kick some serious butt."

"Any last-minute advice before we head to the airport? You worked in the garment industry for years. I really wish you could be there to make me look less incompetent."

Anna sat up straighter and reached across the table, placing her hand on Sarah's. "From the moment I met you, you struck me as nothing less than cool determination. You will have no problem with Sylvia Hodge. She's drawn to people who have a vision. Show her what you see for your future and everything else will fall into place. I promise."

Sarah blew out a breath. What a coup it was to have Anna's help, and Aiden's for that matter. He was bankrolling this venture, after all. But knowing he was putting so much money into it only made the pressure that much more intense.

"Ready?" Aiden strode into the room. In dark gray dress pants and a white dress shirt, he looked so good he could've sold her a magic bag of beans.

Jacob followed, holding Oliver. He'd just had his first diaper-changing lesson, courtesy of Aiden. The former daddy-in-training was teaching the daddy-to-be.

"You look extra handsome holding a baby," Anna said to Jacob, slowly pushing herself up out of the chair.

Jacob flashed his dazzling smile. "It's the ultimate fashion accessory. Women go crazy for it."

Anna rolled her eyes and sidled up next to them. "Don't push it."

Aiden watched Anna and Jacob with Oliver. He was anxious—Sarah could see it. That made a small part of her melt on the inside. There was nothing sexier than a man who was on edge about leaving his child.

For Aiden's sake, Sarah started the goodbyes. "Okay, sweet boy. Anna and Jacob are going to take very good care of you. We'll see you tomorrow when we get back." She kissed his forehead. Emotion washed over her. In a few short days she'd be doing this for real.

"Goodbye, buddy." Aiden's voice wobbled as he cupped the back of Oliver's head and kissed his cheek.

Aiden's driver John was waiting outside in the black SUV, idling at the curb. The ride to the private terminal in Teterboro, New Jersey, took nearly an hour with traffic. Aiden made work calls, leaving no time for them to talk. The way he laid down the law with people was inspiring and intimidating. Would she ever be that in control? Could she grow her company and give herself security, command respect and just tell people what she wanted? She had a hard time imagining she could muster that much mojo.

The car went through a security gate and drove up alongside the sleek white jet, tastefully marked with the royal blue LangTel logo. The plane's boarding stairs had been lowered to the tarmac. Aiden's driver opened the door for Sarah, and she dug her fingernails into the tender heels of her hands, reminding herself that this wasn't a movie. This was really happening. "Thank you so much, John. I don't know how you navigate traffic in this giant car, but I'm glad you can."

"Thank you, Ms. Daltrey."

She gently swiped at his arm. "Please, call me Sarah. It's only fair since I call you John."

An amused smile crossed his lips. "You're very gracious, Sarah. Excuse me while I retrieve the bags. I'll see you on board."

"Oh. You're joining us?"

"I always drive Mr. Langford. Everywhere."

Aiden climbed out of the car and placed his hand on her lower back, only amping up her nervousness. That touch from any other man would've reminded her this was really happening. It would've taken her *out* of the dream. But Aiden? He put her that much further into it. He nodded toward the plane, his sunglasses glinting. "Shall we?"

They climbed the stairs and stepped into the luxurious cabin, piling one surreal moment on top of countless others. There were a dozen or so oversize cream-colored leather seats, mahogany and chrome accents. Everything gleamed—even the flight attendant's red lipstick and white smile as she said, "Welcome aboard."

"Anywhere special you want me?" Sarah asked Aiden.

He removed his sunglasses and cocked an eyebrow. "Wherever you'd like to be is fine with me."

Her face flushed with heat. Damn him and his comebacks. Damn her and her brain that just had to go there. She took the seat closest to her. Aiden took the one directly opposite, facing her.

"May I get you a drink before takeoff, Ms. Daltrey?"

Sarah hadn't had a chance to introduce herself. Nor did she have a chance to respond.

"We'll have the usual, Genevieve," Aiden answered.

"Yes, Mr. Langford."

"I trust that champagne is okay?" Aiden asked Sarah.

"It's nine in the morning."

Aiden ruffled the newspaper open. "You're on edge. I see it on your face."

My face is fine. John boarded, taking a seat in the front. Sarah glanced out the window as the plane began to taxi. She hated to fly and seeing outside after take-off would only make it worse. She lowered the shade, doing her best to act as if this was exactly where she should be. If she seemed on edge, it was because she was as far out of her element as she could imagine, and this was only the start of her day on the brink. There was much more to deal with—Sylvia Hodge, the fashion show, the countless glamorous people who would be in attendance, who would undoubtedly be wondering how someone like Sarah got in. And then there was the not-small matter of spending twenty-four hours with Aiden, when she already didn't trust herself with him.

Own it, Sarah. Own it. "I'm not on edge. I'm just thinking over the things Anna and I talked about this morning. For the moment when I meet Sylvia Hodge." *God help me.* "She gave me some great pointers." Sarah sat up straight and crossed her legs. If only she was in her black pencil skirt, short peplum jacket and pumps, she'd be the epitome of put-together. Thankfully, Tessa had sent that power suit, along with the dress she'd designed and a bathing suit. The clothes would help her fake her way through today, and then she'd be golden.

In the interest of control and modesty, Sarah had been explicit with Tessa about the swimsuit, asking for the plain black one at the very bottom of her dresser. *Plain black. Got it?* Hopefully she could talk Aiden out of a trip to the pool and she wouldn't even need it. She'd seen him without his shirt and managed to keep her own clothes on. No point in pressing her luck.

The flight attendant brought two champagne flutes, filled with golden bubbles. Aiden folded his newspaper and reached out to clink his glass with hers. "To success."

She admired his optimism—success was not a familiar concept. "Yes. I'm hoping for success."

His vision narrowed on her, a crease forming between his eyes. "There is no hoping. You need to walk up to Sylvia Hodge tonight, tell her what you do and tell her what you want. That's how you make deals. By taking charge."

"And how, exactly, do I take charge with Sylvia Hodge? She's a legend. She's put more designers on the map than anyone, and she's probably destroyed more. Just saying her name scares me."

"I can tell. And it's not good. But don't worry. I have a solution."

A solution? "Please. Do tell. I'm all ears."

"How do you feel about heights?"

Uh-oh. Mr. Adventure-seeker was at play here. "Absolutely mortified. So whatever it is that you're planning, just forget it. I'm not climbing or jumping off anything."

"No climbing or jumping. Just fun. You don't have to do anything other than sit there."

"A roller coaster?"

"Parasailing."

"Over water? In the sky?" Sarah's brain sputtered. As if she wasn't already nervous enough. "No way. My hair looks amazing today. I'm not giving up a God-given good hair day."

He leaned closer and rested his elbows on his thighs. "Sarah. You made me step outside my comfort zone. It's time for me to do the same for you. Trust me. It'll be good."

"Maybe I forgot to ask my assistant to send a bathing suit. Oh well. Your plan won't work."

He shook his head. "I was in the room when you asked her. Unless she's terrible at her job, you should be all set. Stop making excuses."

Sarah blew out an exasperated breath, downed half of her champagne and slumped back in her seat. *Great. Now I get to risk life and limb right before I put my entire career on the line.*

Three hours later, they were on the ground in Miami. Sarah stepped off the plane, thick balmy air hitting her skin as she squinted into the bright Florida sun. At least summery weather made it feel like vacation. A black SUV like the one Aiden had in New York was waiting for them planeside. John had them off to the hotel in no time. As much as Sarah felt out of place, traveling with

Aiden did have an upside. No waiting to check your bag or slogging your way through security. It was lovely.

She glanced over at him while the car sped along a causeway, palm trees fluttering in the breeze outside. He was so good-looking it sometimes hurt to set her sights on him for too long, as if her eyes grew weary of handsome. What would it be like to be Aiden Langford's female companion on a trip like this? Romantic female companion. She already knew the VIP treatment was wonderful, but sleeping in the same bed with six-plus feet of pure man? Kissing him, taking off his clothes…the thought of it made her squirm in her seat. She quickly turned away and stared out her own window. She had to stay focused on business, even if romantic fantasies about Aiden were a nice escape.

They arrived at The Miami Palm hotel, situated on a private key, a small island just off the coast of downtown, connected to land by a gated bridge. Inside, the hotel lobby had classic Miami opulence—art deco chandeliers, towering potted palms and a tropical color scheme of cream, coral and sea green. Aiden was apparently a frequent customer—every employee, especially every female employee, knew his name. They didn't even have to check in. The bellman brought them straight up to the top floor. And one room.

"One room?" Sarah said under her breath. "Isn't that a little presumptuous?" It was her duty to feign indignation, at least while her brain attempted to determine what exactly Aiden was up to.

The bellman opened the door and stepped aside. Sarah nearly gasped when she walked into the luxurious space. Heck, if this was where they were staying, Aiden could presume whatever he wanted to. A sprawling living area was before them, with two large sectional couches. A black baby grand piano was beyond that, flanked by linen-upholstered armchairs. A dining table for ten was on the other side of the living area, with a wet bar beyond that. Along the length of the room were a trio of sliding doors leading to the terrace, with palm trees, a cloudless sky and the ocean completing the view.

"The presidential suite, sir." The bellman wheeled their suitcases inside.

Aiden peered down at her. "See? Nothing presumptuous. Two bedrooms. Two master baths. Separated by this big room. And don't worry, your door has a lock."

Now Sarah felt stupid for saying anything. This was a business trip. She needed to start acting as such.

"It's wonderful. Thank you so much for arranging this. I really appreciate it."

"Holding up my end of the bargain."

And nothing more.

"Time to get settled," he added. "We leave in forty-five minutes."

Her shoulders dropped. "So you were serious about parasailing? Really?"

"Dead serious. I don't get to do this sort of thing nearly enough. I'm in Miami, I'm going parasailing. And you're coming with me."

"You know, I'm really more of a lounge-on-the-beach-with-a-mojito sort of girl."

"Although I'm enjoying the vision, that's not the plan today."

"But…"

He shook his head. "No buts. If you get scared, the boat can bring us in. But you won't get scared."

"Fine." Dejected, Sarah sucked in a deep breath and ambled to her room.

Once inside, Sarah's eyes were immediately drawn to her gown, hanging neatly on a dressing rod next to the closet. Her suit coat and skirt were behind the dress. They must have been steamed by the hotel staff. They looked the picture of perfection. The emerald-green silk of the dress was just as exquisite as she'd remembered, the beading on the bodice and trailing down onto the skirt equally sublime. This was a good thing. She would be confident in this dress. It would be her superhero costume, the one in which she set aside her everyday persona and became an invincible woman.

Time to step outside her comfort zone.

She turned, her vision drifted to the bed and her inner peace sizzled away like a bead of water on a hot skillet. *Good God. No.* There sat her beach cover-up, along with her bathing suit. The aqua-blue caftan was great thinking on Tessa's part. Sarah hadn't thought to ask for it. Next to it was indeed her black bathing suit—a plain one at that, precisely what she'd asked Tessa to send. Only that it wasn't the one she wanted. *One-piece, dammit. One-piece. Not the teeny tiny bikini.*

Ten

If Sarah seemed apprehensive during the flight, now she was downright agitated—trudging out of her room dressed for the beach in a pretty blue cover-up paired with sandals and a scowl. The hair that had been perfectly in place on the airplane was in a ponytail. Her makeup had been removed. Sarah didn't wear a lot of it, but there was a difference and he liked the change. It harkened back to the only morning she'd been in his bed, and the way he'd pored over her as she slept, wondering if it was a good idea to pursue any of the ideas ruminating in his head—thoughts of kisses bestowed and returned, and every satisfying thing that it could lead to.

"Ready?" he asked.

"You're making me do something I am literally ter-rified to do. So no, I'm not ready." Clutching her handbag, she plodded toward him as if she'd been banished to the gallows.

He placed his arm around her shoulders and gave her a gentle squeeze while unsubtly ushering her to the door. "You'll feel better after this. I promise."

"What do I get if I don't feel better? What if I feel worse? I'm already so worked up about tonight that I feel like I'm going to lose my lunch. We haven't even had lunch."

"You're just going to have to trust me."

She glared up at him when he opened the door. "You realize it's not my inclination to trust you, at all."

Her freckles again teased him, toyed with him. Now that they were completely alone, he wanted nothing more than to bend down and kiss her. Just get it over with so he could stop thinking so damn much and let his instincts take over. There was nothing stopping them— nothing stopping *him*, except the entirely foreign worry that sex might ruin what was already between them.

"You don't trust me even a little bit?"

"This is a trick question. If I say I trust you, it'll make your argument for letting a thin parachute carry me thousands of feet into the air over the Atlantic Ocean."

"Biscayne Bay. And it's five hundred feet, and that's only if they let us go all the way up. Not much more than a football field."

"Oh."

"I'll be right next to you. You can hold my hand."

"Oh. Okay." The faintest of smiles crossed her lips. "I guess that makes it a little better."

"Good. Let's go before you change your mind."

They headed down to the lobby. John was waiting outside and swiftly had them on their way to their beach adventure. This excursion was about more than distracting Sarah from her worries. He wanted her to see this side of him. She'd remarked about the photos in his apartment, comments that made him think she didn't understand why he did risky things. He hadn't always been the guy who jumped out of airplanes, but once you've done something that you could die doing, it takes away fear.

"I want to say one thing. Part of being successful in business is learning to fake fearlessness."

Sarah removed her sunglasses and shot him a very hot look of admonition. "Fake it? I assumed you were actually fearless. I've heard you on the phone. You're incredibly intimidating."

"I don't have to fake it now, but that doesn't mean there wasn't a time when I was scared to forge my own way."

"But you come from such an influential business family. Surely your dad helped you, even if you didn't have the best relationship."

It was Aiden's natural inclination to steer away from this topic, but Sarah knew his history. "That's one thing my dad offered, but I didn't want his help. By the time I graduated from college, I was too bitter to take anything from him anyway. I wanted to prove to my parents that I didn't need them. Now, granted, I had a trust fund that got me started, that was no small matter, but I did everything else on my own."

"Refusing your dad's help couldn't have made things better with your family."

"It didn't. But I also didn't feel that it was my responsibility to make things better." If ever there had been an understatement, that was it. "Regardless, I was terrified. I didn't know how to find the right companies to invest in or how to influence people. When a friend invited me to go skydiving in Peru, that changed my mindset. I realized that I could do anything because I had nothing to lose."

"Except maybe your life."

He laughed quietly. "Maybe. But when you give up a little control, you find out what you're made of. It's not my intention to scare you. I want to show you that you can do anything. You have no reason to be intimidated by Sylvia Hodge."

"I can think of fifty reasons, easy."

"No. Listen. You have a vibrant concept, you've demonstrated there's a demand for your product and most importantly, you have you. There's no substitute for a smart, creative mind. That brain of yours is pure gold."

Sarah's eyes swirled with wonder and emotion. Exquisite and teary, they took Aiden's breath away. He'd played a role in her reaction and that made his heart thump wildly.

"You make it sound like I can't fail."

"I don't think you can." Aiden blanketed Sarah's hand with his, unable to keep from touching her. He really did believe in her. After all, she'd found a way to reach him when he'd been determined to keep her away.

She turned her hand, allowing their palms to touch, wrapping her fingers around his. Her grip said that she didn't want to let go. Neither did he. Her skin was too soft, too warm. He'd waited too long for this. He had to know where this single touch led.

"Mr. Langford, the boat you hired is waiting. Anything I can carry out to the dock for you?"

John's voice yanked Aiden out from under the spell of Sarah. They were already in a parking lot adjacent to the beach.

"We'll be just fine, John." Even with the disruption, Sarah hadn't let go, and neither had he. Was his heart about to leave his body via his throat? Sarah was giving him a glimmer of hope he wasn't sure he should cling to. Why he was in any way unsure of himself with Sarah was a mystery. With any other woman, he knew precisely where hand-holding led…into his bed. With Sarah? They might never share more than what they just had.

They hiked across the hot white sand, sidestepping people soaking up the midday rays. The crew was waiting for them on a shiny blue speedboat, bobbing in the water. The winch, which held the line for the sail, was all set up on the back. Aiden greeted the young man standing sentry on the dock, introduced Sarah and helped her aboard.

"Here are your life jackets." An older man handed a red one to Sarah and a larger blue one to Aiden.

Sarah placed her handbag on one of the benches lining the perimeter of the hull. Aiden removed his T-shirt and put on the life vest. His eyes connected with Sarah's— she'd been watching, again filling him with ill-advised hope. She turned her attention to getting her flowing cover-up sleeves through the armholes of the life jacket.

"You should get rid of the top layer," he said.

She blew out a breath. "Yeah. Okay."

She tossed the vest aside and turned her back to him, suggesting she wanted privacy. But this gave him the perfect chance to watch. The aqua fabric skimmed the backs of her toned legs, over her pleasantly round bottom, revealing the feminine curve of her waist, and the beautiful contours of her back and shoulders. With string ties at the back and at the hips, her bikini left little to the imagination, but his mind was racing to fill in the details. Blood rushed to the lower half of his body. Heat surged. Again.

She turned and sat on the bench as the boat puttered from the dock. Aiden wasn't sure he could sit alongside her and keep his hands to himself, so he kneeled on the bench, steadying himself with his hand. Ocean air rushed as the boat picked up speed, cooling his overheated skin.

The crew prepared the harnesses and called Aiden and Sarah over. Even with the boat jostling them as it bounced over the waves, it wasn't hard to see Sarah's nervousness. Her back and shoulders were stiff as a board as she stepped into the straps and they hooked her onto the winch. Aiden took his place next to her, the two of them sitting on the platform at the back of the boat. One of the men released the chute. The wind caught it, yanking on the line.

Sarah grabbed his thigh. "Oh, my God. I'm going to die."

No. But I might. He swallowed hard and took her hand. "We're in this together."

"What a comforting thought," she yelled, as the boat gained speed.

One of the crewmen leaned in closer, grasping the top bar carrying the harnesses. "We're sending you up now. Give us a signal if you decide to come back down. Have fun."

The boat engine revved. The winch creaked. The rope began to unwind and they were lifted to standing.

Sarah yelped and squeezed his hand even harder. "Don't let go," she screamed as their feet left the deck and they were carried up into the air.

The line unrolled, steadily carrying them up into the warm, cloudless sky above the crystalline sea. She'd never before wondered what it felt like to be on the end of a kite string, but this had to be what it was like, floating free while tethered to safety. As they reached a height that she'd been sure would terrify her, elation bubbled up from the depths of her stomach, giving way to breathy giggles.

Aiden laughed. "You okay?" he yelled, still holding her hand.

"Yeah," she shouted. She did have to work at focusing on the freeness of the moment, rather than the fact that she and her feet were dangling hundreds of feet above the bay. She'd never willfully experienced a height like this, outside of visiting the top of the Sears Tower in Chicago and pressing her forehead against the window for a second before she clamped her eyes shut. Somehow, the tautness of the rope and the tug of the chute made it feel as though they couldn't fall. Or perhaps it was Aiden. He did scary things all the time and he always lived to tell the tale.

Careful not to look straight down, she took in the view—high-rise hotels lining the beach, people dotting the sand and countless shades of beautiful blue composing the vista of sea. She sucked in salt air, relished the wind against her skin, and more than anything, the comfort of Aiden's hand.

If someone had asked her a month ago if she'd ever do this, she would have said no way. Now she had to wonder why she'd never allowed herself to try. Bungee jumping was definitely not on her list, nor was BASE jumping or skydiving—basically, jumping of any kind was out of the question. But this—flying in the air with a handsome, hunky guy holding on to her? *This* she could do.

Aiden was such a huge part of everything she was feeling right now. He'd been so sweet in the car, giving her the pep talk that helped her step back from the proverbial ledge. Even though they were only friends, they'd grown close, and she couldn't help but compare him to other men. Aiden, even when he made her question what she was doing, did not doubt her ability to rise to the occasion. So many men had dismissed her, especially Jason. Not Aiden. He thought of her as more. That made her see those things in herself.

She smiled. Bad memories would not dog her today. Today was full of possibility. Today was about taking risks. Aiden leaned into her, sending a zap of electricity through her. It made them pitch to one side, which made her heart race. Sarah angled toward Aiden and that became their game, back and forth, laughing, smiling at each other, shoulders touching, hand in hand. Her heart swelled with the way she felt right now—unhindered. She could do anything today.

It was hard to know how long they'd been up in the air, but all too soon the rope was pulling them back to earth. Without much trouble, their feet settled on the boat's landing pad, while the crew rushed to bring in the sail and help them out of their harnesses. Minutes later they were at the dock and trekking back across the sand to the spot where John was waiting.

Taking her seat in the car with sandy feet, windswept hair and the blood brought to the surface of her skin, Sarah's nervousness had been obliterated. Feeling invincible and exhilarated, she wanted to hold on to this moment forever.

Aiden handed her a cold bottle of water, which John had brought for them. "So?"

She smiled, turning away from him for a moment and watching South Beach whiz by as they headed back to the hotel. She knew the answer Aiden was waiting for. He wanted confirmation that he'd been right and she'd been wrong. Part of her didn't want to give it to the guy who always got whatever he wanted, but he'd earned it.

She turned back. "You were right. I loved it. It was scary at first, but I loved it."

"And how are you feeling about tonight?"

She took in a deep breath through her nose, waiting for the old nervousness to creep back in. She was on such a high that she couldn't fathom that old negativity. She could do what she set out to do. She was going to dazzle Sylvia Hodge tonight, impress her with her gown, the photos she had ready on her phone, and prove to her that her company was worth investing in. "Honestly? I feel great. Which is scary in its own way since it's not normally the way I feel, but definitely better than the other kind of scared."

"A little bit of scared keeps you on your toes, but you can get rid of the rest of it. It doesn't help you accomplish what you want." He took a swig of his water and screwed the cap back on. That little bit of time in the sun had darkened his skin, giving it a golden glow, making him that much more touchable.

"You tan quickly."

He removed his sunglasses and lifted his T-shirt sleeve, revealing the rounded curves of his muscular biceps. "I guess I did get some sun." He glanced over, setting his sights on her, making her feel exposed in a wonderful way. "You did, too. Your shoulder is pink."

Sarah turned her head. Her cover-up had slipped down and she did indeed look sunburned. "Oh, man. And I used SPF 700."

"They make such a thing?"

She shook her head. "I'm exaggerating." She examined her other shoulder, the one that had been closest to Aiden and shaded by the chute. "This side is fine."

"We'll take a look at it when we get back to the room."

We will?

"I don't want you uncomfortable tonight. I want you to walk into that room in that dress and slay everyone."

The thought of slaying a room full of people was laughable. "You do realize I'm short, right? Room slaying is more for a woman who's five foot ten."

"All that matters is that you have confidence. And I have complete confidence that you will look stunning."

Sarah swallowed, hard. The man was lethal. Her resolve was doing more than melting away—she was having a hard time remembering why she'd ever needed it in the first place. Would it hurt anyone if she and Aiden gave in to a night of passion? She'd promised herself she'd stay away from single dads if she were caring for their children, but maybe this was different. She and Aiden had already shared so much more than she ever had with Jason. And she wasn't really Oliver's caretaker. Not for long, at least.

They arrived at the hotel and rode to their floor, both quiet. Considering all of the very sexual thoughts running through her head, Sarah was terrified to open her mouth.

"We have about an hour until we need to leave. I'm going to go ahead and hop in the shower." Aiden took his shirt off right there.

Sarah nearly choked. "Okay." She couldn't have moved if she wanted to. Not when the world's most gorgeous display was right before her. Considering that she'd never touched it, she had an irrational attachment to his chest, longed to spread her fingers across it, feel his skin against her palms and soak up the glory of Aiden Langford.

"Before you get in the shower, let me check your

back for sunburn. I'm worried about that shoulder of yours."

"Oh, okay."

She stepped closer so carefully you'd think she was about to feed a lion from the palm of her hand.

"Turn around."

Goose bumps dotted her skin. He swept her pony-tail to the side and teased her beach cover-up from her shoulder with his finger.

"Anything?" Her voice squeaked.

"I can't see very well. Take off this thing."

No no no. No taking off of things. Oh, but she wanted to. She really, really wanted to. He was so close, radiating heat right into her back. He towered behind her, making her wonderfully aware of his size. She crossed her arms, curled her fingers under the hem of the caftan and lifted it over her head.

"Much better."

She swore his voice was tailor-made for the bedroom. *Why is it hotter now that I'm wearing fewer clothes?*

He placed one hand on her left shoulder while brushing the right with the tips of his fingers, leaving behind a trail of white heat. His touch was heavenly and perfect. She could have stood there forever and let him ever-so-slightly caress her shoulder. "You're a little pink, but I think you'll live."

That's rich since I feel like fainting. "Okay. Thanks."

Eleven

Sarah finished her makeup—a few dabs of powder and another swipe of deep red lipstick. "I can do this," she muttered. "I was born to do this." *I think.*

She took a final look-see in the full-length mirror. Was this dress the right call? It was certainly stunning. And if any garment, aside from a Kama nightgown, could tell the story of her design aesthetic, this was it. Still, with a neckline aimed straight for her navel, it was a bold statement. For Aiden, it was practically a lie detector test. If he showed no interest while she was wearing it? She'd know precisely how stupid her thoughts about him had been. Like most things she designed, the dress was meant to be left in a puddle on the floor at the end of the night. It was meant to leave a man with few defenses.

Not that she had a single guard against Aiden. If he made a move, it'd be painful to say no. It didn't help that her brain wouldn't stop obsessing on the blissful moment when he'd caressed her shoulder and only their bathing suits had kept them apart. What would he have done if she'd glanced over her shoulder and uttered the words she'd been dying to say? *Kiss me.*

Some part of her hoped that he wanted her the way she wanted him. Another part—the grumpy, sensible part—said that it didn't matter. Crossing that line would be foolish. It would never end well. He was worldlier and infinitely more powerful than any man she'd been with. How could she possibly make an impression on a man like Aiden? How could she not disappoint him with her relatively narrow frame of reference in the bedroom? And if it happened, and proved to be a misstep, there would be many awkward conversations to endure over the coming days. All while she was trying to save her business.

It was best not to push her luck. There were only so many things she could conquer in one day—Sylvia Hodge and building a fashion empire at the top of today's list. She needed to force herself to stop barking up the handsome billionaire.

Sarah grabbed her evening bag and marched into the living room. Aiden was standing near the door, talking on his cell. Even seeing him only in profile, he was too much to take in with a single look. So her vision landed on his black dress shoes, perfectly polished. Eyes traveling north, she savored every inch—his long legs in black tux pants, his heavenly torso in a crisp white shirt, topped off with an untied bow tie. However ludicrous the thought, she considered begging him to forget the Sylvia thing. Face time with a fashion icon? Who cared? She needed face time with him. Face-to-face. Lips to lips.

He turned, his vision unsubtly washing over her. "I need to go," he said to his phone, then tucked it into his pocket.

Sarah waited for his verdict, her pulse racing and her mouth dry.

"You look absolutely gorgeous," he said. "The dress is stunning."

The dress. The dress is stunning. She couldn't ignore his choice of words.

"You clean up pretty nice yourself." She stopped short of mentioning that his suit pants might look better draped over a chair, his shirt flung over a lamp.

He cocked an eyebrow and tied his tie without so much as looking in the mirror. Surely her heart was never meant to withstand these flirtatious blows. "Good?" he asked.

"Your tie?"

"Yes."

"It's a little crooked." He'd done a spot-on job, but this was too good an excuse to touch him. She set down her bag and straightened the tie, quickly learning that with her height disadvantage, she was giving him a bird's-eye view down the front of her dress. His warm smell teased her nose, making the proximity of his mouth impossible to ignore. Why was she torturing herself? She patted his shoulder and stepped back. "You're perfect." *Too perfect.*

"Good. Let's get out of here."

John quickly had them to the warehouse where Forward Style was being held. The show moved from city to city each year, and to make it that much more exclusive—and elusive—the exact location was never revealed to guests until hours before it started. Judging by the jam of limousines and expensive cars in front of the venue, along with the mass of people and photographers standing behind barricades, Sarah could only imagine the mayhem if the address were publicized ahead of time.

Sitting in the car, waiting for their turn at the red carpet, Sarah's earlier calm faded. The closer they crept, it got worse. Cameras flashed. Spotlights beamed into the night sky. Sarah's pulse acted like it was auditioning to join a Miami music rhythm section. This world they were about to step into was all kinds of intimidating, but she'd wanted this since she was a teenager. *You've waited long enough. This is your future.*

A valet opened the door and Aiden was out first. Sarah scooted across the seat, and just when she had another pang of doubt, he took her hand and gave it a squeeze. Regardless of what it meant, she was so glad to have her fingers safely tucked inside his grasp. He didn't have to give a speech to bolster her now. His touch was all she needed.

She'd worried that the photographers' camera flashes would stop when she stepped out of the car, but they kept coming. Of course, it was part of the excitement of the evening, or quite possibly the allure of Aiden, but she soaked up every second. She stood tall and smiled, hanging on to Aiden's hand just as she had in the air above Biscayne Bay.

Across the threshold, gorgeous women in supershort dresses offered glasses of sparkling wine. Aiden and Sarah filtered into the warehouse, which had been done up with glitzy lighting and cascades of white fabric hanging from the tall ceilings. A din of conversation and thumping dance music filled the room. Models, designers, rock stars and the Hollywood elite were decked out in a dizzying array of fashion choices—everything from priceless gowns to ripped jeans. They all seemed to know each other, embracing, laughing and chattering away.

A handsome young man in a tux offered to show them to their seats. As they walked up the aisle, Sarah couldn't believe it as they got closer and closer to the front. They stopped at the first row, taking their seats between one notorious magazine editor and renowned twin sister fashion mavens. "How'd you manage these?" she whispered in Aiden's ear.

He put his arm around her and nestled his nose in her hair. "I made an additional donation. I figured it would add to your mystery. Everyone will want to know who you are."

Sarah looked up at him, their lips only inches apart. With every crazy thing going on in this room, hundreds of endlessly wealthy and fabulous people milling about, she could only think about planting her mouth on his. Earlier, she'd wanted him just for being his sexy self.

Now she wanted to kiss him for countless reasons. "I don't know what to say. Thank you."

He smiled. "Of course."

The music faded and there was a rush for people to take their seats. The song changed to a delicate instrumental and a hush fell over the crowd. Sarah's heart threatened to explode. This was really happening. Out strode a grinning Sylvia Hodge, lithe and graceful in a silvery-gray gown with a slit up one leg. Her black hair was pulled back in a high ponytail, her wrist weighed down with a stunning collection of diamond bangles. She carried herself as a woman who had the world at her feet. And she did, so it worked.

She raised a microphone to her ruby-red lips. "I want to thank everyone for joining us for this year's Forward Style. It's much more than a fashion event— it's a community coming together to support a worthy cause. This year, all proceeds benefit art programs in our public schools. That makes me incredibly proud. We must nurture creativity whenever possible. Speaking of which, I know you're all ready to see what our brilliant designers have in store for us this evening. Without further ado, on with the show." Sylvia worked it on her way backstage, hips swaying, hemline flapping around her ankles.

The music changed to another driving dance beat, and before Sarah could put a single thought into Sylvia, the show started. An endless line of models filed down the runway as the secret Forward Style collections were revealed. Sarah focused on design details, following along in the program until she noticed that none of the other VIPs were doing the same. She set aside her guide. An up-and-coming designer wouldn't be obsessing over who made what, she'd be enjoying the creativity of her peers. She sat straighter, watching the show, keenly aware of two people—Aiden right next to her and Sylvia, now seated in the front row on the opposite side of the catwalk. One person to be her rock, the other her greatest challenge.

After an unbelievable display of fashion, the show drew to a close with the designers' curtain call. The crowd gave a standing ovation, furiously clapping. Sarah kept her eyes trained on Sylvia. Once the final bows had been taken, it was time to act. *Goodbye comfort zone.*

"I'm going in," she blurted to Aiden.

Surprise crossed his face. "Yeah. Go."

Sarah pushed her way through the throng of people, easier said than done when you're height challenged, but she was not about to be thwarted. *Just fake it.* When she reached Sylvia, she didn't think. She acted. She touched her arm and started talking. "Ms. Hodge. I'm Sarah Daltrey and I need to tell you about my company, Kama. I know you're shopping for new brands and you need to see my designs. My company makes women's sleepwear and lingerie. There's a gap in your company's portfolio when it comes to that category."

Sylvia looked both astonished and amused. "Not many people have the nerve to be so direct with me. Can you show me your work?"

"I'm wearing one of my own designs tonight."

Sylvia quickly eyed the dress. "Okay. Show me more."

Not a ringing endorsement, but Sarah still couldn't get out her phone fast enough. She pulled up the gallery and handed it over to Sylvia, then began explaining each image. That was the easy part. And now that she'd gotten over her initial nervousness, every word out of her mouth became more natural.

Sylvia flicked back through the pictures a second time, nodding, as Sarah tried to interpret what each facial tic might mean. She returned Sarah's phone then gave her a business card. "Call my office tomorrow morning and ask for Katie. She'll walk you through what else we'll need from you before we can talk any further. I trust you have your financials in order? A website? Designs for next season?"

Sarah's mind whirred into gear. This was happening. "Yes. Of course. Katie. I'll call her."

"She gets in very early. I'd call before her day gets too busy. You have talent, but it won't do you any good if you don't find the right partner."

Sylvia Hodge, who Sarah now regarded as a powerful and intimidating fairy godmother, disappeared into the crowd.

"Well, that was intense," Aiden quipped. "You just did it. You didn't need my help at all."

Sarah grasped his elbow with one hand and his lapel with the other. She wasn't sure she should be so forward, but taking what she wanted and faking it when necessary had actually worked. "But I did need your help. Now let's get out of here. This music is making me crazy."

They made a quick escape into the Miami night, heading back to the hotel. Sarah settled into her seat—

as much as a girl can when she's floating on air for the second time in one day.

Aiden turned to her. "If things don't work out with Sylvia, I want to invest."

"Fashion's not in your wheelhouse, remember?"

"Sarah, you could sell me the Brooklyn Bridge right now. That was a really tough thing you did. And you killed it."

Pride swelled inside her, as did her yearning for Aiden. However much she'd wished earlier that she could touch him, kiss him, run her fingertips over the intricate patterns of that tattoo on his arm, the desire was tenfold now. "You're so sweet."

"That's not what you'd say if you knew the thoughts going through my head when I look at you in that dress."

"Thoughts?"

Her face was on fire. Swallowing became an impossible task. *Kiss him. Just get it over with and if he turns you down, you can tell him it had been a momentary blip of insanity.* The car came to a stop. *Why are we not moving? We need to get to the hotel. Now.*

"We're here, Mr. Langford," John said.

"Good." Aiden gazed deeply into Sarah's eyes, taking away her ability to breathe, let alone think. "Time to retire for the evening."

Halfway through the lobby, Sarah was overcome with the feeling that everything was about to change. And not just with her career.

Aiden unknotted his tie on the elevator. He couldn't take it anymore. He'd started something in the car, something that was not smart, but he'd had enough. Being with Sarah all day had been too great a test. Every inch of her was temptation…he would've berated himself for suggesting parasailing and subjecting himself to hours with her in a bikini if he hadn't so greatly enjoyed it. He'd thought at least a dozen times about untying one of those bows on her bathing suit, caressing her soft skin, leaving her bare to him.

Next to her in the elevator, the view was incredible, but looking was no longer enough. He needed to touch her, without the dress, needed her in his bed, so he could finally get lost in her sweetness and beauty. He'd be kissing her right here and now if he thought for even a minute that he'd be able to stop.

Finally, mercifully, the elevator reached their floor.

Sarah stopped halfway down the hall, planted her hand against the wall and kicked off her shoes. "These things are killing me."

Aiden laughed quietly. Her career was built on aesthetics, but she wasn't afraid to be real with him. He opened their door, ready to sweep Sarah into his arms and finally just kiss her.

She had other plans. "Sorry, but I need to do one thing."

Before he could say a single word, she darted into her room and closed the door.

Well damn.

He stood there for a moment, unsure of what to do, which made no sense. He almost always knew what to do. *Come on, Sarah. Hurry up.* But she didn't appear. And there was no sign that she would return. What could she possibly be doing in there? *How long could it take?* So that was that. He'd crossed a line with that comment in the car, and it hadn't worked. Time to admit defeat.

He stalked to his room and closed his door, disappointment threatening to consume him. This was not the way things typically went for him. Hell, he couldn't think of any time this had happened. Then again, he'd never known a woman like Sarah. He stepped out of his pants, which oddly enough made his arousal a more pressing matter. It felt good to be less constrained, but now it was impossible to ignore how badly he wanted Sarah. *Should I go to her? Tell her how badly I want to make love to her? Or will I seem like a jerk?* They only had a few more days together.

A quiet knock came at his door.

Aiden looked around the room, unsure if it was a construct of his imagination. A second knock came. He lunged for the door and opened it, pure evidence of how little he was thinking. In his boxers, there was no hiding how thrilled he was to see her.

"There you are," she said, slightly breathless, in the tempting black-and-silver nightgown.

"Where else would I be?"

"I thought you would wait for me. I mean…after the car. It seemed like you wanted to, um, spend some time together." Her eyes flashed with something he'd never seen, which was saying a lot since she was such an animated woman.

"I do want to spend time together." Why couldn't

he find something smooth to say? Oh right, everything below his waist was doing the thinking.

"What are you up to?" She looked everywhere—at the ceiling, the floor, the windows with the view of the water. Either she was trying to ignore the erection in the room, or she was waiting for him to make his move.

"I'm up to this." He leaned down and cupped the side of her cheek, placing a soft and tentative kiss on her lips. He choked back a sigh of relief. He'd wanted this more than he'd known.

She popped up on to her tiptoes and reached for his neck. Before he could think twice about what she was doing, she had him in the throes of the most enthusiastic kiss anyone had ever laid on him. He stooped to get closer, her lips wild and untamed, as if she'd been sent to consume him. For an instant he had to wonder if he'd fallen asleep and was stuck in a dream, but then she nipped his lower lip and the heavenly sting brought him to the present.

"Do you?" He wasn't sure what he was trying to prove by inquiring about her intentions. They were pretty clear.

She drew in a deep breath and nodded, never taking her eyes off him. "I do. I want you to take off my nightgown and kiss me again. I want you to touch me. I need to touch you. And I don't want to stop until we're both exhausted."

She gazed up at him, her eyes open and honest, while he teased one of the skinny straps from her shoulder. The corners of her sweet lips turned up when he reached for the hem of her gown and tugged it over her head, dropping it to the floor.

He couldn't have stifled the groan in his throat if he'd wanted to. Having her stand before him, completely naked, was overwhelming. He didn't know where to start—he wanted every part of her at once. Her breasts were even more beautiful than he'd imagined—full and luscious. The outline of her bikini showed from their time in the sun—stretches of creamy, touchable skin paired with the golden glow of her tan.

He snaked his arms around her waist, leaning down to kiss her, taking her velvety bottom into his hands. Was he the luckiest man ever right now? He'd been fantasizing about this five minutes ago and now it was actually happening.

He wanted to kiss her in a way that projected how badly he wanted her, but their height difference made it difficult. He turned and sat on the edge of the bed, pulling her along. She stepped between his knees, her body bracketed by his legs. In his eyes, she was the embodiment of luscious femininity. His arms reined her in, holding her close, as his lips traveled from her pouty mouth to her neck, down the center of her chest, and he took her pert nipple into his mouth as he plucked at the other with his fingers. He listened to the way her breath halted, took note of the subtle moves she made to get closer to him. He had so much to learn about what pleased her, and about what would make her unravel.

She dug her fingers into his hair, massaging his scalp, soft and sexy moans coming from her gorgeous mouth. She dropped to her knees, seeking another kiss from him as she pulled at his boxer briefs and forced him to pop his hips up from the bed, so she could slide them down his legs. Kneeling before him, she took his length in hand, stroking firmly, making contact with her riveting gaze. It was everything he could do to hold his head up, let alone keep his eyes open. Her touch was bringing every nerve ending in his body alive, much as she was changing his entire life, bringing positive energy that hadn't been there before. She lowered her head and wrapped her lips around his tip, taking him into her warm and welcoming mouth. Aiden had to recline back onto his elbows—the way the blood was rushing through his body right now was enough to make him pass out.

She took her time with him, sweet and sensual with every pass, placing one hand flat on his stomach and caressing tenderly. The tension was coiling inside him like a rattlesnake about to strike. He couldn't hold on much longer.

"Sarah, come here."

She made a gentle popping sound when she released him from her mouth, but she kept her hand firmly wrapped around him. "I thought you were enjoying yourself."

The sight of her full mouth, her fingers on his body, her luscious curves, made it nearly impossible to form a coherent thought. "I was. You have no idea." He sat up and cupped the side of her face. "But I want to make love to you." His lips trailed from her mouth to her cheek and again down the graceful sweep of her neck. "If that's what you want."

"Aiden, I've wanted you from the moment I laid eyes on you. So, yes. That's what I want."

Did she really mean that? Aside from a few moments of flirtation, and the time he'd caught her staring after the bath with Oliver, he'd assumed the attraction was somewhat one-sided. Most women were very up-front with him. Sarah had hidden it well. How she somehow managed to become even sexier to him was beyond him, he only knew that this particular revelation did exactly that. Not many people surprised him. Sarah did.

"I have a condom in my suitcase," he said.

She climbed up onto the bed and rolled to her side. "Hoping to get lucky in Miami?"

He smiled to himself and shook his head. "That wasn't what I was thinking. I just happen to have them with me when I travel."

"Best to be prepared."

"Yes." He presented her with the foil packet and cocked an eyebrow. "Care to do the honors?"

"I do." The flirtation in her voice was enough to send him sailing past his peak, until she touched him. Then it was as if he were clutching the crumbling edge of a cliff with his fingertips.

She lay back on the bed and he followed, settling between her legs, sinking into her. He bestowed kisses on her forehead, her cheek and then her lips as they rocked together. For someone so small, Sarah had a lot of power resonating from her hips. She was already gathering around him, which made thinking too great a demand, so he didn't bother. He brushed her hair back from her forehead, enjoyed the feeling of her heels on the backs of his thighs and her hands roving up and down the channel of his spine.

Their gazes connected in the soft moonlight filtering through the window as she reached her peak, her body tugging on him in pulses as she gasped for breath. He loved that blissful look on her face—so incomprehensibly beautiful. He gave in to the pleasure, steeped in the knowledge that he'd made her happy. He dropped to his side and she didn't hesitate to curl right into him. They fit so wonderfully together and he couldn't wait to have her again. He was damn lucky to be with her, even if they might never have more than one perfect night.

Twelve

Sarah wasn't sure she'd ever been so tired. Nor had she been so blissfully happy in her own skin. There in Aiden's bed, half-asleep in the early morning light, she replayed her favorite moments with him. The most captivating memory came when Sarah had gotten up in the middle of the night to use the bathroom, only to find him wide-awake when she returned. He hadn't let her get more than a few steps before she was in his arms, his hands roving everywhere as his mouth explored hers and he led her back into the bathroom.

The shower was magnificent—marble and glass, with enough room to play. Hot water covered them in a deluge but there were moments when she could've sworn the heat all came from Aiden's hands. He spread soapy suds across her breasts, and gave her kisses that hardly let her come up for air, all as steam swirled and for the third time in twenty-four hours, it felt as if she were floating.

The man was a magician, every move born of some innate ability she didn't understand. He was always a step ahead of her, anticipating. She never asked for a thing, but again and again he did exactly what she would've asked for if she'd had the guts to put it into words. He'd asked her to sit on the shower bench, then dropped to his knees before her. He hitched one of her legs over his shoulder, and brought her to heights she'd never seen. She was accustomed to being the giver, not the receiver. Sitting back and letting Aiden take control had been heavenly.

But of course she'd begged to return to the role she relished, the one in which she pleased, as it was his turn to sit on the bench and his fingers combed through her hair as she took his steely length into her mouth. Judging by the extended string of dirty talk, which ended only when his body froze and he reached his apex, she'd made him happy—very happy. That turned her on more than anything.

The mattress bounced when Aiden shifted his weight and rolled away from her. She fought disappointment that it hadn't been his body's inclination to seek hers while they were in bed, but perhaps that was for the best. Now that it was morning, and the high of yesterday had faded, reality was creeping back in. She was going home on Sunday. Aiden and Oliver would be starting their new lives then, too. That was as it should be, precisely what she'd come to New York for. She'd done her job; she and Aiden had had their fun. Aiden was not the settling down type. He needed his space—he'd said as much. Becoming a dad was already an awful lot of settling down for a man who needed his freedom. More than being used to those things, he needed them the way everyone else needed air and water.

She'd promised herself she wouldn't get attached or involved. That she wouldn't cross that line with Aiden, however badly she'd wanted him. So that was her one mistake. She'd given in to the way he drew her in. Now it was time to return to their old dynamic or tempt fate. One mistake was forgivable. Two would be idiotic.

She gently peeled back the sheet and sat up, glancing at the alarm clock. It was only a few minutes after five. Best to let Aiden sleep. She could shower and get dressed, pack her things and be ready to go whenever he was. Careful not to disturb the bed, she tiptoed to the other side to get her nightgown. But the sight of that black silk against the pristine white carpet was a snapshot from her painful past—nearly an exact replica. It sent an avalanche of hurtful memories crashing through her head—the morning after what became the final time with Jason, when she'd scrambled through the pile of clothes at the foot of the bed, desperate to find her nightgown and her dignity. That was the morning he'd scoffed at the notion that "sleeping with the nanny" meant anything. It was the morning he'd laughed when she'd said *I love you.*

She closed her eyes, willing the tears away. *You're stronger than this. It's not the same. You can stop be-*

fore you get in too deep. Walk away. That chapter was gone. She'd turned the page.

She picked up her nightgown and crept out of Aiden's room. What happened in Miami stayed in Miami. That was the only way this was going to work.

Aiden woke to an empty bed. He even rolled to his side to touch the spot where he was certain Sarah had been last night. The sheets were cold, as if she'd never been there. He propped himself up on one elbow and raked his fingers through his hair, scanning the room for evidence he wasn't dreaming. But last night had happened. He and Sarah had made love. More than once. It wasn't his mind weaving a fantasy. It had been real.

He sat up to see if his clothes were where he'd left them. They weren't. They were draped over the arm of a chair. Most notably, her nightgown was missing from the floor. *Huh.* He'd made graceful exits from trysts. It'd never happened to him, but Sarah had a habit of keeping him on his toes. Luckily, there were only so many places she could be. He pulled on a clean pair of boxer briefs and began his search. He didn't need to go far.

"Morning." She spoke from behind the newspaper, seated at the dining table, a cup of coffee next to her. "I hope it's okay I ordered breakfast. I was starving and I figured we should get on with our day."

He rubbed his eyes and wandered over to her, struggling to make sense of this version of Sarah. This wasn't at all how he'd expected their morning would go. "You're already dressed and everything."

She didn't look up, eyes trained on the paper. "Packed and ready to go."

Sure enough, her suitcase was parked next to the front door. "You realize we can leave whenever we want, right? The jet will be waiting whenever we get to the airport. There was no need to rush." *I was hoping for some morning sex to start my day.*

"We have a lot to do today. I already spoke to Katie in Sylvia's office. We have a call this afternoon at four. I also called the nanny agency and told them we need more candidates to interview today. It's Thursday, Aiden. There's only so much time until I go home."

Well then. Aiden was used to being the distant one the morning after, the one who made it clear all roads ended here. He respected the tack Sarah took, even if it didn't add up. He'd been sure she was the girl who liked morning cuddles and romantic remembrances of the night before. Apparently not.

There was only one conclusion—her business was her top priority. He'd be a hypocrite to let that bother him. She'd had her big break and it was of her making. She'd be a fool to lose focus, even if they'd shared what he believed to be a special night.

It still didn't sit well with him, although he couldn't discern why. What was this uneasy feeling in his stomach? The one that made him want to take her hand and say sweet things. What was the feeling that made him hope she'd say sexy things in return, flutter her lashes and deliver a proposition he couldn't refuse with her unforgettable lips? *Should we go back to bed?*

He pulled out a chair and took a seat at the table,

pouring himself a cup of coffee. Caffeine might help him find clarity.

Sarah finally made eye contact. "No shirt at the breakfast table?"

Was he in some alternate universe? "You were fine with me not wearing a shirt last night."

She cleared her throat and folded up the newspaper, casting it aside. "That was last night. Today is today."

"Okay, well. I don't feel like getting up and getting a shirt. So you'll have to put up with my chest. Hopefully you can control yourself."

She rolled her eyes. "I'll manage."

This was so stupid. He didn't put up with crap like this. "Did I miss a memo or something? Did we not enjoy ourselves last night? Did I do or say something wrong?"

She downed the last of her orange juice and folded her napkin. "Of course we enjoyed ourselves. It was nice."

Nice?

"But it's time for me to get back to work." With that, she got up from the table.

Aiden grasped her arm. "Okay. I get it." Touching her was a bad idea. He was overcome with that unfamiliar feeling again. It made him want to say things he'd normally never say. *Can we talk? What are you thinking?* What was wrong with him? Too much sun? "You're right. We need to get back to New York to take care of the nanny situation."

"The clock is ticking."

"It is." He let go of her arm, now struck with the feeling that *not* touching her was the bad idea. He needed to get his head on straight. He was not himself this morning. "Give me a few minutes to scarf down some breakfast and read the sports page, then I'll hop in the shower and we can be out the door."

"Do you want me to call John and let him know we'll be ready in a half hour?"

Talk about being in a rush. "Tell him forty-five minutes." He watched her walk away. She wasn't wearing her usual sundress and sandals. Today, she was all business—a straight black skirt and tailored jacket with heels. She looked every bit the role of take-charge entrepreneur. And maybe that was all she wanted to be.

His interactions with Sarah didn't improve over the next several hours. Not in the car on the way to the airport, not on the plane, not in the car back to the apartment. Aiden wasn't sure what he wanted from her—something more than a minimal acknowledgment that they'd shared a fantastic night? He hated the thought of wanting that or needing it, but he did. He had this need for her approval that he'd never experienced before. He needed her to say that she'd enjoyed it—even though he was certain she had. More than a small part of him wished that she'd say that she wanted to do it again. He'd been right to worry that sex would ruin their friendship. And for now, he had to focus on salvaging it.

Of course, his deadline with Sarah loomed. Ten days had seemed like a long time the day she walked into his office, but it had gone so fast. There was so much left to do, especially after the paternity results were back tomorrow. First to tackle was the nanny situation, which Aiden wasn't looking forward to revisiting.

They arrived back at his building midafternoon.

"I just got a text from the nanny agency," Sarah said. "They're sending one more candidate over at three."

"One? That's it? You'd think that with the money I would be paying that there would be more options than one more."

"Between your standards and mine, the pool is limited. Plus, it takes time to find a good nanny. And we don't have any." Sarah put on her sunglasses and climbed out of the car.

Aiden grumbled and followed, not wanting to chase after her, but he had to—she was walking at a clip. "Do you mind telling me what's going on? You've been weird since last night and I don't like it. If we need to talk about something, then please let's do it so that the next few days can be tolerable."

"I don't want to talk about it on the sidewalk. Can we wait until we get upstairs?"

John was blazing his own trail up the walk with their suitcases.

"Yes. Of course." Aiden turned and stopped him. "You know, John. I've got this. Why don't you knock off for the rest of the day? I'm sure you'd like to spend some time with your family." Aiden took the luggage.

"Sir?"

"Is there a problem?"

"No, sir. None at all. I just…you've never sent me home early before."

"Some things are more important than sitting around

waiting on me. I realize it's your job, but I also just took you away from your family for a night. If I need to go anywhere, I'll get a cab."

John shook Aiden's hand. "Thank you so much, sir. I appreciate it. I'll be here bright and early tomorrow morning."

"Great. I might go into the office for a few hours." *It'll keep my mind off the paternity test.*

Aiden bid John his farewell and caught up to Sarah in the lobby. They rode in the elevator in silence. He didn't want to launch into everything right now anyway. He was looking forward to seeing Oliver too much and he didn't want to be in a bad mood when that happened.

His normally quiet apartment was noisy when he and Sarah stepped off the elevator. Music was playing and there was laughter, too—Oliver and Anna both, from the sound of it. Aiden left the suitcases in the entry, in search of the fun. He found them in the library. Jacob was lying on the floor, holding Oliver by the waist above him, letting him drop a few inches, and quickly catching him. Oliver unleashed peals of giggles, as did Anna, who was sitting next to Jacob on the floor. They were oblivious to Aiden and Sarah, too stuck in their happy world.

Aiden was overcome with a feeling impossible to label—longing, regret, sadness and joy. He loved seeing Anna and Jacob like this. He loved hearing Oliver's laugh. He loved seeing what a family looked like against the backdrop of his own home. It gave him an entirely different lens through which to see his future, a view that filled him with optimism and yet there was a nagging sense that not all was right. There were pieces missing. Aiden not only didn't know how to find the pieces, he didn't know what to look for.

Anna turned and her face lit up. "Look who's home, Oliver. It's Daddy."

Tears welled in his eyes. *Daddy. That's who I am now.*

Jacob got up and handed over Oliver, who snuggled right into Aiden's chest. "We had a great time, Aiden. You have an awesome little boy here." He helped Anna get up from the floor.

"You had a good time?" Aiden asked Oliver, rubbing his back and breathing in that magical baby smell.

"He had the best time," Anna said. "He's such a good baby."

Oliver tugged the sunglasses threaded on Aiden's shirt, smearing them with his tiny fingers. Aiden didn't care that they were five-hundred-dollar shades. He merely took the chance to kiss Oliver's temple and hold him close.

Sarah peeked around Aiden's shoulder. "Hey, sweet pea," she said.

Oliver's face lit up, and an elated gurgle rose out of him when she went in for a kiss. They rubbed noses, mere inches from Aiden's face. Sarah's soft, musical laugh filled his ears. Something deep inside him wanted to hold on to that moment forever. Disappointment washed over him when it ended.

Sarah was a missing piece. And that piece was leaving on Sunday.

Thirteen

As every minute passed, it became more difficult to be with Aiden. Sarah had entered territory she'd vowed to avoid, and she'd been a fool to think she could step out of it by adopting a steely demeanor. She could convince her brain of a lot of things, but it didn't mean her body was going to be on board. Just sharing the same air made everything harder—it only made her want him more.

The apartment buzzer rang. "That must be the final nanny," Sarah said to Oliver, scooping him up.

Aiden emerged from his office, where he'd been working. "What's this one's name? Lucy?"

His voice dripped with doubt, saddling Sarah with the fear that he'd turn down their final option. If he did, *he* could deal with the repercussions. Oliver was his responsibility, not hers, and she wasn't going to stay because Aiden refused to make a decision.

"Her name is Lily. Her credentials are exceptional. I think she could be the one."

"I read her résumé, Sarah. You don't have to keep selling me on these people."

Sarah choked back a frustrated grumble. If he were going to sabotage this, he'd better be prepared for a lecture when Lily left.

The elevator doors slid open and Lily roved into the foyer. Her wavy auburn hair was past her shoulders, barely tamed. She wore a swishy orange skirt that grazed the floor and a white tank top—not the professional interview attire Sarah expected. Maybe Aiden wouldn't have to ruin this. Maybe Lily would. "Langford residence?"

"It is. I'm Aiden." He stepped forward to shake her hand. "This is Sarah. She's been filling in as nanny until we find a permanent replacement."

His choice of words stung, especially after what had happened last night. It was confirmation of the way he saw her—as a temporary fixture. "Hi," Sarah said. "This is Oliver."

Lily's eyes grew impossibly large and she tilted her head as she went to him, taking his tiny hand. "Hello, Oliver. Aren't you the cutest thing ever?" Her voice was pure fairy-tale princess—full of magic.

Oliver was immediately taken, going to her.

"If it's okay with you," Lily said, "I'd like to play with him while we chat. I'm not big on formality."

Sarah never would've deigned to dictate the course of

an interview when she was nannying, but she couldn't argue with Oliver's reaction to Lily. He was infatuated, babbling away and tangling his fingers in her hair. Aiden gestured for them to go into the library, where many of Oliver's toys were spread out on the floor.

Lily plopped down on the rug and jumped in with playtime. "I assume you've seen my résumé."

Aiden sat while Sarah stood, observing. "It's impressive," he answered. "You've worked for some very high-profile families."

"I've been lucky to have had the chance. And every child I've ever cared for has been wonderful. It worked well with those families because they appreciated my approach to nannying."

"And how would you describe that?" Aiden asked.

"Well, of course I'm firm with the children. They need some boundaries. But otherwise, I believe in letting them take the lead. If we go to a museum, we do what the child wants to do. If we do an art project, we make a mess if that suits the child's disposition. If we go to the park and he wants to dig in the dirt rather than play on the swings, we do that. We'll sing songs at the top of our lungs and splash water in the bathtub. Kids need freedom and space."

Sarah was taken aback. She'd never managed to deliver a spiel on her former vocation so eloquently. If it was rehearsed, it didn't come off that way. Then there was her choice of words—freedom and space. Aiden would have to reach to turn down Lily.

He sat forward and rested his elbows on his knees. "What else can you tell me?"

Lily launched into more of her philosophy of child-rearing, walking him through her typical weekly schedule for a toddler. She talked of long walks and afternoons in the park, of play dates and visits to the library.

Sarah had to step away as visions of Lily's plans appeared in her head. Oliver would have a wonderful, idyllic life and he'd be well cared for. It was everything she'd come looking for. If Aiden hired Lily, it would mean that Sarah had succeeded—she'd honored Gail's wishes and found Oliver his forever home. So why did she feel so empty? Why did it have to feel as if she were looking out the rear window of a car as it sped away?

"Sarah, can I speak to you for a moment?" Aiden's voice worked its way into her psyche, her weakness for him harder to ignore with his presence.

She sucked in a deep breath and shoved aside her feelings. "Yes, of course. What's up?"

"Am I crazy or did I just find a nanny? Lily is perfect."

She smiled and nodded, fighting her irrational tears. "I agree. She's fantastic. You and Oliver will be very happy with her. I think you should offer her the job." It was best to keep pushing him away, or else her heart would be a pile of rubble by the end of the weekend.

"Okay, then. It's decided." Not wasting a second, he strode into the library while Sarah followed. "Lily, I'd like to offer you the job. Can you start first thing Monday morning?"

Lily smiled awkwardly. "Oh. The agency should've told you I have another offer on the table right now. A family that's moving to France. I haven't decided yet if I'm going to take it or not. I promised them I'd decide before the end of the weekend."

"Whatever they're paying you, I'll double it," Aiden said.

Aiden was clearly committed to moving forward. Sarah reminded herself this was supposed to make her happy.

Lily got up from the floor. "I appreciate that, but it's not the money. Honestly, it's the chance to travel."

"I love to travel. I'd love to take Oliver on adventures all over the world and you can come with us."

Sarah could imagine the three of them globetrotting together. Talk about feeling left out...

Lily cast her sights down at the baby. "He's so sweet and you make a compelling case. If it's okay with you, I'd still like to have the weekend to think about it. I know you need someone on Monday, but the other family wouldn't need me to start for another month, so I could at least take over from..." Lily glanced at Sarah and pressed her hand to her chest. "I'm so sorry. I've completely forgotten your name."

Sarah blanched. *I'm so out of the picture I'm a ghost.* "Oh, no worries. It's Sarah."

"I could take over from Sarah until you find a permanent replacement."

"I guess I can't ask for much more than that," Aiden said. "But please, think about the things I said. I'm sure you and Oliver are a great match."

Lily bid her farewells, which included several sloppy

kisses from Oliver. Even the baby was practically ready to send Sarah on her way.

Aiden let out an exaggerated exhale as the elevator doors closed. "I'm so relieved that's worked out, at least for the next month. I didn't want you to think I was trying to hold you hostage. I just needed someone I felt good about."

Sarah nodded. "I'm relieved, too." *And feel so much worse.*

"Now you can go to Boston on Sunday." He strolled into the kitchen and poured himself a glass of water. "Actually, you could go home earlier if you wanted to. The paternity results are in tomorrow and they're sending over the legal team to take care of the paperwork. You could go home Saturday. I mean, if you're eager to go."

Seriously? Sarah felt as though her heart should just throw up its hands and stomp out of the room. It hadn't even been twenty-four hours since they'd slept together and he was shooing her out the door? Her instincts that morning had been 100 percent correct. She needed to get out, not get wrapped up in the guy who hated the idea of being tied down. "Okay. I'll leave as soon as it makes sense. Speaking of which, I have that conference call with Katie in a few minutes. I'll take it in my room." Tears threatened again, but she had to keep it together. She turned to the stairs, but Aiden stopped her with a hand on her forearm.

"Sarah, wait."

She froze, the warmth of Aiden's fingers searing her

skin. *What? Did you change your mind? Do you actually want me to stay through Sunday?*

"Use my office for your call."

Aiden wasn't sure what had gotten into him when
he'd told Sarah she should leave before Sunday if she
wanted to. It had seemed like the generous thing to do,
but now he was kicking himself, even though he had to
let her go sometime. Her actions suggested she hadn't
wanted more than one night with him, and from the
very beginning, she'd been laser-focused on the deadline. She'd delivered everything she'd promised. He'd
done the same. Once the paperwork was done, their relationship could come to its logical conclusion. Except
that Aiden had that uneasy feeling in the center of his
chest again, the one that said something was wrong. He
couldn't shake it, no matter how hard he tried.

Aiden played with Oliver in the library, unable to
ignore how badly Sarah's call was going. She hadn't
closed the doors to his office, so he couldn't avoid hearing her say things like, "I don't know. I'll have to get
that together for you." Sylvia Hodge and her cohorts
would likely only sink money into someone who was
flawlessly prepared. He had to force himself to not walk
in and offer his help. He'd done his part. He'd put her
in the room with Sylvia Hodge. It was up to Sarah to
make this happen.

Aiden's worst suspicions were confirmed when
Sarah drifted out of the office. All traces of the excitement she'd had yesterday were gone.

"Well?" he asked.

"I feel like I just got hit by a train." Her voice was weary, as if she couldn't take another step.

"Those calls can be like that. It's not always a bad thing." He didn't want to give her false hope, but he couldn't stand to see her like this. Her upbeat air was gone and he missed it.

She pursed her lips and shook her head. "No. This was bad. There were so many questions I couldn't answer."

"I thought your financials were in order."

"They are, but they asked me things like what percentage of the market I can corner and how quickly I can do it. I can't answer that. That's what I need them for."

Aiden's stomach sank. Should he have prepared her more? Had he dropped the ball? "It's okay to not know the answer to everything."

"Judging by what Katie said, it's not. She said they don't work with companies that aren't as up-to-speed on the business end as they are on the design end. That's me, Aiden. I know the design end. I stumble through the rest of it."

"But you've accomplished a lot. They'll see that. And there's the value of your concept and product. I'm sure that it's Katie's job to be a bulldog, so Sylvia can step in and be your savior."

"I don't know why I tried to do any of this. Sylvia probably only agreed to have her people talk to me because I had her cornered and she didn't want to make a scene."

"Don't be so defeatist. You haven't had a definitive

answer yet. And if this doesn't work out, you'll move on to the next thing. I've done it many times."

Sarah's jaw tensed in a way Aiden had never seen, not even that first day in his office when she'd been so frustrated. "There is no next thing, Aiden. I'm not you. I don't have a million amazing possibilities to juggle at one time. This is it for me. My career, my life, my paycheck. There's nothing else for me but this. This is the one thing I'm good at."

"Besides nannying."

"I don't know how many times I have to tell you that I'm done with that. Forever."

Yes, Sarah had said these things to him before, but he still didn't understand it. "Did something bad happen? Is that why you're so adamant about not going back to nannying?"

"Yes, something bad happened. Why else does a person decide they can't do something anymore?"

"Why didn't you tell me?"

"I don't talk about it with anyone, especially not someone I've known for a week."

Her dismissiveness felt like someone choking his heart. A week. In some ways it felt as if he'd known Sarah his whole life. "I'm just trying to help."

"I can't tell you. I'm too ashamed."

Now he *had* to find out what had happened. Sarah, ashamed? He couldn't imagine her doing a single dishonorable thing. "I'm not going to judge you. But I'd like to know what's going on. I think I've earned an explanation."

She stared at the ceiling, blinking back tears. "I got

fired from my last job. I've never been let go in my entire life, and this family meant the world to me. It destroyed me. I took one more nannying job after that, but I only lasted a day. I had to do something else. I couldn't go back."

"So you were really attached to the children?"

"Child. Singular. A little girl named Chloe. She was a few months older than Oliver." She cast her sights down at the baby and pressed her lips together solidly. "I can't talk about this, Aiden. I really can't."

He pulled her into his arms, breathing in her sweet scent, overcome with the memory of how good this had felt last night. They fit together well. "It's okay to tell me. Maybe you'll feel better if you get it out. That's what you told me the night we sat up on the terrace and I was still upset about my mom."

She settled her head against his chest, trembling. "I became romantically involved with my boss. I fell in love with him."

"Go on." He choked back his discomfort at the thought of her with another man.

"I knew it was wrong, but I was so drawn to him and I adored his daughter and it just happened. His wife had passed away before I was hired and he seemed to need me and care about me, but I read the whole thing wrong."

He caressed her arm, closing his eyes and drawing in a deep breath. Her anguish poured into him. He longed to take it away. He also needed to know more. What kind of monster was this man who'd captured her heart and thrown it away? "What happened?"

Sarah looked up at him, but he didn't let go. He wanted her to know that he was there for her. "I told him the truth. I told him that I loved him. He actually laughed at me. He thought I was kidding. He thought we were having a fling. He'd assumed that I'd done it before, but I hadn't. And when I told him that it wasn't a joke, he fired me. He didn't want me around his daughter. He said he couldn't trust me anymore. Do you have any idea how awful that felt?"

"He couldn't trust you because you loved him?"

"Yes."

"That's horrible."

"It's the worst thing that's ever happened to me. Unrequited love is one thing, but it's quite another to have your bond with a child stripped away. I've always cared deeply for the children in my charge. I never knew another way. Leaving was always the hardest part, but at least it'd always been on good terms. This was just solid rejection. I was hollowed out. That's why I don't nanny anymore."

Oliver crawled over to them and pulled himself to standing with the help of Aiden's pant leg.

Sarah picked him up, tears streaming down her face. She smoothed his hair back and kissed his cheek. "I'm sorry. I know this is way more than you ever wanted to know about me. But now at least you know why Kama means so much. I can't go back to my old life."

Aiden had started over many times. He knew the appeal of a new beginning. "I understand. Completely."

She sighed and managed a smile before she handed over Oliver. "Thank you. I appreciate that. Now I need to go upstairs and regroup and try to figure out how I salvage this Sylvia Hodge thing. Are you okay to do bedtime on your own?"

"Yes, of course. I'm sure you want some alone time anyway." He really hoped the answer was that she didn't want to be by herself, that she wanted to stay up and talk after Oliver went to bed.

"I do. I need some time to think. Plus, a few more nights and you won't have me around to help. You might as well start acting like I'm not even here."

Fourteen

Sarah was working feverishly on an email to Katie and Sylvia Hodge Friday morning, when Aiden strolled into his home office, phone in hand. He grinned like a man without a single worry.

"Probability of paternity is 99.9 percent. Oliver is mine."

Sarah jumped out of the chair and raced from behind the desk, throwing her arms around him. "I knew it. I just knew it."

Unfortunately, the instant she was pressed against him, her body wanted to stay, especially when he returned the embrace with a firm squeeze, rocking her back and forth. With the clock ticking, should she take these happy moments? Even when they'd haunt her later?

"I knew in my heart that he was my son, but I don't

think I realized how much it would mean to have the confirmation. Considering my own history, this gives me peace. Oliver and I are a family. No one can take that away from us." Aiden released her from their hug. It was impossible to ignore how enticing he was when he was so relaxed. Good news suited him well. "The lawyers will be by in an hour to do the final paperwork. They'll have it before the judge this afternoon. Then we'll be done."

Done. She was so close to being done, it wasn't even funny. She'd worried about awkward conversations after sleeping together, but Aiden hadn't said a thing. She respected a man who followed her lead, but part of her really wished he'd fought her on it beyond his minor protestation in Miami. His ready acceptance was another reminder that in the end, she was just another woman. Nothing more. "All sewn up. No more loose ends." *It's for the best. And you know it.*

He cleared his throat and walked over to the bookcase, straightening a book. "Have you thought at all about when you'll want to go?"

If only he knew how much that question hurt. "I'd like a little more time with Oliver." *And you, if I'm being honest.*

"I'm asking because I was thinking about having my family over tonight. For a celebration. Officially welcome Oliver into the Langford family. I definitely want you here for that."

Sarah could breathe a little easier. Maybe she was at least a notch above the other women he'd been with. "I'd love to be there. I think it's great you're involving your family. It's important to mend fences with your mom."

"This gives me another perfect opportunity to push her on it, but tonight's probably not the night, huh? Not when everyone is here."

"Agreed. Tonight should be happy. Leave the tough conversation for another day."

He turned to her while a soft smile crossed his face. "It means a lot to have someone to talk to about this."

Sarah grinned, even when she was dying a little more on the inside. Their ability to discuss painful things was one of the best parts of their friendship. He'd been so sweet with her when she'd opened up about Jason. He hadn't judged her. Not at all. "Good. I'm glad."

He knocked the bookcase with his knuckle. "I'll leave you to whatever you were working on. I'm going to get a workout in before the lawyers come by."

The afternoon was a flurry of activity. Documents were signed. Calls were made to the market to have food and drinks delivered. Oliver got an early bath before his first Langford family gathering. Sarah relished the hustle and bustle. It kept her mind off the clock, a constant reminder that it would soon be time to not only say goodbye to two people she cared about deeply, but after that came do-or-die time with Kama. What if everything with Sylvia Hodge blew up? Because that's where it seemed to be headed. The email she'd sent that afternoon had been answered with yet more questions. More doubts. More reasons they might say no. Then where would she be? Back in Boston, alone, her future a big fat question mark.

Aiden's brother Adam and his wife, Melanie, were the first to arrive. Adam was incredibly charming—

just as magnetic as Aiden, with a smile that was nearly identical. That gave Sarah pause. Maybe Evelyn Langford wasn't keeping a secret. Sarah didn't have much time to think about it though, quickly hitting it off with Melanie, who was both down-to-earth and talkative.

"I have to say, Aiden. Fatherhood really agrees with you," Adam said as Oliver sat happily in Aiden's arms.

"Thank you. I really appreciate that." Aiden's response was more than polite conversation. His brother's kind words had resonated.

"I'll have to get some pointers from you when the time comes. Mel and I are trying to get pregnant," Adam said.

Melanie's eyes flashed. She swatted Adam on the arm. "I thought we weren't telling anyone."

Adam put his arm around her and pulled her closer, kissing her on the cheek. "We're with family. There are no secrets."

If only that were true with the Langfords.

Jacob and Anna arrived, both ecstatic to see Oliver. The baby had apparently fallen in love with his uncle Jacob during the Miami trip, since he readily went to him. Everyone chatted in the kitchen, wine and cocktails flowing, music in the background. No problems. No controversy. But despite Aiden's pledge to keep things light, Sarah had a sinking feeling that might change with the arrival of the final guest.

Aiden grabbed a carrot stick from a platter of veggies and dip. "Leave it to my mother to be late for her grandson's first party."

"Maybe she's stuck in traffic." Sarah arranged crackers on a plate.

"You know she likes making an entrance," Adam said. "It's annoying, but true."

The apartment buzzer rang. Aiden took in a deep breath and adopted the most forced smile Sarah had ever seen. "Mom's here." He soon returned with Evelyn.

She greeted everyone sweetly, saving Oliver for last. "There's my handsome grandson."

Oliver was content to stay with Jacob, but he humored his grandmother, laughing when she made a silly face and holding her finger with his pudgy hand.

Aiden smiled, but Sarah could see once again that he was having to try. What it must be like to live with something so big hanging over your head—Sarah could only imagine. It burdened him, greatly, and how could it not? It had made him the person he was today. Nothing was safe from the influence of the secret he was convinced his mother was keeping.

For nearly two hours, Sarah dedicated herself to being a comfort to Aiden, bringing him a fresh drink when needed, offering a reassuring smile or moment of eye contact, especially when he sat on the living room sofa with his mom. Every time he acknowledged Sarah with a smile or a nod, it shored up their solidarity. The friendship they'd forged would be one of her greatest takeaways from their ten days together. It could comfort her when she found herself wondering what would have happened if she hadn't put up a stone wall after Miami.

"How are you holding up?" She crouched next to him at the end of the couch when his mother had gone to use the bathroom. Things were winding down, which was good since Aiden seemed to have reached his limit. His eyes were tired, his jaw tense, brows drawn tightly together.

"She's making me crazy. She's spent the whole night planning things for Oliver's birthday next month and talking about how she wants to spend Christmas morning with him. It rubs me the wrong way. I can't help it."

Probably because she never did those things for you. Sarah bit down on her lip to keep from saying what Aiden already knew. "Maybe she's trying to make up for the past."

A slight smile crossed his face and he clasped his hand over hers. "You're so sweet. I love your optimism. But I'm pretty sure this is just her way of sweeping the past under the rug."

He was probably right. She didn't know why she had the need to put a positive spin on his mother's insensitivity, she only knew that she did. "So let's just get everyone to clear out."

"Yes. Oliver needs to get to bed anyway."

By the time Aiden's mom returned from the bathroom, he'd had enough for one day. Sarah was right. Everyone needed to go home. He got up from the couch. "I don't want to spoil the party, but I need to get Oliver to bed."

His mother smiled and nodded. "Such a good dad." She popped up onto her tiptoes and kissed Aiden on the cheek. "It's been a wonderful night. I only wish your father could've lived to meet his grandson."

That image left Aiden frozen with the words he wanted to say. It would be easier on everyone if he let it go, but after years on the periphery of his family, doubt festering in his head and heart, he not only wanted the truth, it was the only thing he could speak. "I'm not sure he would've accepted Oliver." *He sure as hell didn't accept me.*

"Of course he would have."

Again, the need—the thirst—for the truth was desperate. The fire inside him, the pain he lived with every day, blazed. "But he didn't accept me."

His mother's eyes were horror stricken. "Your father loved you."

Aiden calmly confronted her by looking her square in the eye. "Just tell me. I'm tired of wondering. I don't want to have to think about it anymore."

"But…"

He clasped his hand firmly over hers. "Mom. I love you, but there is no *but*. If you want to be a part of Oliver's life, you'll tell me the truth about who my father is."

Adam approached. "Everything okay?"

Aiden refused to let his mother off the hook. "Mom was going to finally tell me the truth about who my dad is. Weren't you?"

"You'd keep my grandson from me?"

Aiden nodded. "If you love me, you'll tell me."

His mother's eyes misted. Her lower lip trembled. "I don't want to hurt you. I never did."

"Mom, it's too late. This is your chance to start making it better." Aiden braced for what was to come.

His mother perched on the edge of a chair. "We tried to make it work, but your father…" She cast her eyes up at Adam, then Aiden. Anna joined them and took Aiden's hand, squeezing it tightly. "Your father couldn't deal with it. He looked at Aiden and all he saw was what he perceived as betrayal. That's why you were sent off to school. And I agreed, because I couldn't watch him be cruel to you and loving with Adam and Anna. Your father had such a temper. I was worried about what might happen if he got truly angry at you. That's why you were sent away."

Aiden swallowed, dogged by lonely memories from his childhood—birthdays in boarding school, phone calls from his mother where she acted as if this was all normal and summers at home as the odd man out. He was an expert at filing those things away, but he had to face them now. *This is it. The moment I've waited for.* "Then who's my father?"

Jacob, holding Oliver, had joined Anna. Melanie had crept closer, too, standing with Adam. They all had each other. Who did Aiden have? He turned and his vision landed on her—Sarah, standing there with concern painted on her face. She was his one true ally in this room.

"Your uncle Charlie is your biological father. I dated him before Roger. It was short, but that's when you were conceived. I lied to Roger when we first started going out. I didn't want him to know that I'd been with his brother. Roger and I fell in love and when we learned I was pregnant, we got married." She peered up at Aiden. The corners of her mouth were drawn down, deep creases between her eyes. She might be hurt, but she'd left him with the same scars. "It didn't take long after you were born for Roger to put two and two together. You have the same birthmark on your leg that Charlie had."

"The same one Oliver has." Aiden was amazed he'd said anything calmly considering the speed at which his mind and heart were racing.

"Yes." She gathered her composure. "Things were okay for a while, but everything changed when Adam was born. He always compared you two. He and Charlie had such a contentious relationship, it was no big surprise. And then Charlie died in the motorcycle accident and Roger couldn't handle it. It was such a tangle of emotion and you were the one it all got directed at, Aiden. I had to get you somewhere safe, where I knew you'd be okay. That's why I agreed to send you off to school."

Aiden stood there, thinking. With everything that had been launched at him, his mind was remarkably clear. The truth had washed away the dirt on the windows. He could see. The anger hadn't left, but it made sense now. He turned again to Sarah, who was standing back from the group. Of all the people in that room, she was the one he wanted to talk to. She was the one he wanted to confide in. He wanted to be alone with her. He wanted to feel good again. As to whether she wanted the same from him, he had no idea. Her face showed only sweet empathy as he walked Oliver over to her.

"I'm going to send everybody packing," he said softly.

"Good," Sarah said.

Aiden turned to his family. "Thanks everybody for coming today. It's been good for Oliver. And for me."

"Say something," his mother pleaded. "Please tell me you forgive me."

He could've been so cruel, but it wasn't in his heart. However misguided she might've been, she'd thought she was doing the right thing. "I forgive you, Mom. That doesn't mean I'm over it. We're talking about a lifetime of lies. It will take time. Someday I want you to tell me more about my real dad. For tonight, I think it's best if everyone goes."

Adam reached out to shake Aiden's hand. It might've been the first time that Aiden felt zero ill will toward his brother. They'd both been caught in the same dysfunctional dynamic. Adam might've reaped some of the good things, but he'd had his own burdens.

"You're my brother, Aiden," Adam said. "And I love you. I'm around if you need to talk about this."

"I'd like that," Aiden replied.

"I'm not sure what to say," his mother said. "Other than goodbye."

"Why don't we plan on you coming over next week for some time with your grandson?" Aiden answered. It was time for the healing to begin.

"I would love it." With that, Adam walked his mom and Melanie to the door.

Anna grasped Aiden's arm, tears in her eyes. "You were right," she muttered. "I didn't want to believe it. I'm so sorry."

He hugged his sister. "Don't apologize. You've never been anything but loving and supportive. You know, you're going to make such an amazing mom. I can't wait for Oliver to have a cousin."

Anna smiled through her tears and pecked him on the cheek. "I love you."

"I love you, too."

He walked Anna and Jacob to the entryway and watched as they stepped onto the elevator with Adam, Melanie and Evelyn, the door sliding closed. There were footsteps behind him. He knew it was Sarah, and not because she was the only other adult in the house. In only a week, he'd learned the tempo of her gait.

"If you want, I can do bedtime tonight," she said. "I'm sure you're exhausted."

Her voice was salve to his soul. He turned and it felt as if the universe was presenting him with the cure to all that ailed him. Whatever the problem, she made things better.

"Let's both put him to bed. Together."

"Oh. Sure. I'd like that."

The party had taken it out of Oliver. Aiden put him in his pajamas and Sarah read him a story, sitting with him in the rocking chair. Aiden leaned against the door frame, studying them together. If only he could capture that moment in a bottle, save it for later, after she was gone. Sarah's absence would leave a void in his and Oliver's life that would be impossible to fill. But it was what she wanted. She'd made that clear.

After only a few minutes, Oliver sacked out in Sarah's arms. She gently set him in the crib, and she and Aiden tiptoed into the hall.

"I'm sorry about tonight." Aiden reached for her arm.

"I know we said that I should wait for another time, but I had to say something. It was killing me."

"I'm proud of you for doing it. Even though it hurts right now, be patient with yourself. Give yourself some time to process it. And in the end, Oliver's love will heal you. I truly believe that."

He would have smiled if it weren't so hard to breathe. She was so determined to make everything better, and that made her even more beautiful, that much more impossible to resist.

"I think I'll head to bed," she said. "I'm sure you want time to think about everything."

Could he risk his pride for a second time tonight? He had to. Even if she might say she didn't want him the way he wanted her. He might not get another chance. "Don't go, Sarah. Stay with me."

Fifteen

Stay with me. Sarah wasn't sure she'd heard his words correctly. They were surprising. They were scary—driving her to a place where she surrendered to her deep longing for him. Did he want her? She wasn't about to make presumptions about what Aiden had said. Not now. Not when she'd be opening herself up to more hurt. "Did you want to talk?"

He granted the smallest fragment of a smile, looking at her with his heartbreaking blue eyes, his gaze saying he didn't need to talk. He tenderly tucked her hair behind her ear, drawing his finger along her jaw to her chin. "I don't know what force in the universe brought you to me, Sarah. I only know that right now, I need you. I want you. And I'd like to think that you want me, too."

The air stood still, but Sarah swayed, lightheaded

from Aiden's words. Their one night together had been electric, filling her head with memories she'd never surrender, but judging by the deep timbre of Aiden's voice, they might shatter what happened in Miami. "I don't want to ruin our friendship." *And no-strings-attached only breaks my heart.*

"Is that why you shut things down after Miami?"

"Yes." It wasn't the whole truth, but it was enough. As much as sleeping with Aiden might be a mistake, she didn't want to deprive herself of him. Would one more time really hurt? "And I've spent every minute since then regretting it."

"Then I say we have no more regrets."

Before she knew what was happening, he scooped her up into his arms. She'd never had a man carry her anywhere. Her small stature had always made her wonder why—apparently she'd had to wait for Aiden. She wrapped her hands around his neck and leaned into him. He took the few steps necessary to cross the threshold into his room. He set her gently on the bed and stretched out next to her.

She cupped the side of his face, the stubble of his beard scratching her palm. Her heart beat a frantic rhythm as she waited. Then his lips were on hers, soft and sensuous, and that made her pulse race faster. She closed her eyes to immerse herself in the world of Aiden—the silky soft sheets and his masculine smell, his solid, muscular body. He palmed her thigh, his hand inching along under her skirt, sending ribbons of electricity through her.

He rolled to his back, taking her with him until she

was straddling his hips. Her dress was now hitched up around her and Aiden explored beneath her skirt again, slipping his fingers into the back of her lace panties and cupping her bottom. She rested her arms on the bed above his shoulders and dug her fingers into his thick hair, rocking her pelvis against his, his rock-hard erection rubbing against her apex. The need for Aiden had been building for two days, and everything he did made it more pronounced—his tongue exploring her mouth, his white-hot touch.

She sat back and scrambled her way through the buttons of his shirt. He untucked it, then shifted and rolled his magnificent shoulders out of his sleeves. She sat there in awe, reaching out and skimming her fingers along the contours of his shoulders. He was so incredible, inside and out. He clutched her neck, and brought her mouth back down onto his as she again rolled her hips, grinding against his crotch, making everything between her legs blaze with licks of fire—each pass was a tiny measure of gratification, and a bigger dose of torment. She needed him now.

"Touch me, Aiden."

She reached behind her and unzipped her dress, then Aiden threaded his hands beneath the skirt again and pushed the garment up over her head. She planted her hands on the bed next to his shoulders, and he traced the edge of her bra cups with his finger, dipping below the fabric edge and rubbing her nipple. The skin contracted hard beneath his touch, and goose bumps followed. A deep moan left her lips, just to let off a bit of the pressure. He was torturing her, his gaze never leaving her, the need in his eyes fierce and undeniable. He slid his finger under the strap and nudged it off her shoulder, then did the same on the other side. She was about to beg him to take off her bra when he snapped the clasp and the garment fell away. He cupped her breasts in his strong hands—such blissful relief that you'd think she'd waited a lifetime for his touch. She arched her back and her eyes drifted shut as he raised his head and flicked his tongue against one nipple, need shuddering through her. His lips closed on the tight bud, while his hand trailed down her stomach and slipped down the front of her panties, finding her apex.

His fingers teased, touching lightly, drawing gasps from her lungs as he took full control. She settled her forehead on his shoulder as he masterfully brought her closer to climax with firm circles and a steady pace. The pleasure rose inside her, cresting. The tension would build, then ebb, then surge back until she was again at the very edge. When it finally became too much and she gave way, she smashed her mouth into his shoulder to quiet her cries of ecstasy.

But now she only needed him more. She climbed off him and watched as a sexy grin crossed his face when she unbuckled his belt and unzipped the zipper. Not having the fortitude to tease him, she slipped his pants and boxers down at the same time. He was so primed it nearly stopped her dead in her tracks. She appreciated the dark, lusty expression on his face as she wrapped her fingers around him and stroked firmly. He watched for only a moment before his eyes drifted closed and his shoulders let go of all tension. She leaned in and pressed her lips against his, loving the way the depth of his kiss told her how much he appreciated each pass of her hands. His skin was so warm and smooth, but the pressure beneath the surface was intense. Pleasing him like this was so gratifying, but she needed him fully. She needed him to make love to her. She wanted them joined that way again.

"Aiden, make love to me."

He rolled to his side and ran his fingers through her hair, covering her face with kisses. "I want to. Now." He sat up and opened a drawer in the bedside table, handing her the condom packet. She tore it open as he stretched out again. He drew in a sharp breath when she rolled it onto his waiting erection. Then he watched as she slipped off her panties and kicked them to the floor when they were to her ankles.

He positioned himself between her legs when she lay back on the bed. "This is virtually the only thing I've thought about since we got back from Miami."

"Really?"

"Really."

He guided himself inside as she pulled his hips down and he sank into her, her body molding perfectly around him. He lowered his head and they settled into a long and tangled kiss. They moved together in their perfect rhythm, rocking back and forth as the kisses became more frantic, less refined. His breaths were ragged and shallow and it was clear he was close to climax. He reached down between them and placed his thumb against her center until she came and he quickly followed.

He collapsed next to her, catching his breath.

She was floating back down to earth, her mind a

whirl of wonderful things. "That was incredible." *But I want more.*

He smiled, his eyes half-open. "I hope you aren't too tired. I want to make the most of our time together."

Make the most of it. Her thoughts, exactly.

In the new light of morning, Sarah again watched Aiden sleep. She lay on her side, one arm tucked under her pillow, studying his face, notably calm after last night. Aiden had let his guard down. He'd let her in and it had all been his idea. She hadn't had to push for a thing. She felt like a new person, emerging from her dark cocoon in the nick of time. One more day and she'd have been gone. Now, leaving was unimaginable. She'd be crumpling her own heart into a tiny ball. Certainly Aiden wouldn't let her. Their connection was too strong.

The events of the last week had turned everything upside down, but that meant she was out from under the menacing cloud, the one that had followed her for more than a year. Even more remarkable, the saddest thing she could imagine, Oliver losing his mother and Sarah losing her friend, had brought happiness. She could see a life with Aiden. She could imagine becoming Oliver's mom if that was where she and Aiden chose to take things. They could be a family.

There were still obstacles to overcome and the most pressing was no small thing—saying those three little words. But after last night with Aiden, riding out the aftereffects of a secret he'd feared his entire life, they'd cemented their bond. So as frightening as it was, she would take the leap of telling him her true feelings. When she'd sworn to never say it first again, she'd had no way of knowing that a man as extraordinary as Aiden would come into her life. He was different. They had a foundation. Synergy. There would be no sad ending after *I love you*.

Aiden shifted in the bed, scrunching up his face and groaning quietly. He snaked his arm around Sarah's waist and pulled her against him. "You're so far away."

She smiled as her eyes drifted shut and she inhaled his heady smell. "I'm right here."

He smoothed his hand over her bare bottom, gently squeezing. "So you are. My mistake." He nuzzled his way into her neck and she granted him access, even though it usually brought a fit of squealing. He peppered her skin with kisses that started soft and tentative but were now deeper and longer as their bodies pressed together.

"I usually don't like it if someone kisses my neck. After last night, you can kiss me wherever you want."

"It wasn't just last night. Earlier this morning was noteworthy, too."

She laughed quietly, but arched her back and hitched her leg up over his hip. Just thinking about it made her want him again. "It was wonderful."

He clasped her face and planted a kiss on her lips. "Thank you for everything last night."

"It's a little weird to say thank you for sex."

He shook his head and nudged at her nose with his own—such a sweet and tender gesture, it left her breathless. "No. I mean everything before we ended up in bed. You're just..."

She didn't want to be holding her breath, but she

couldn't help it. Was he about to confess his feelings? Would he take her worry away and impart those three little words first?

He scanned her face, his eyes searching for something. "You're a miracle. I don't know how I got so lucky to have you and Oliver walk into my life, but I'm thankful. You've been there for me and I'm so appreciative."

She smiled wide, even though he hadn't relieved her of her greatest fear. "I like being there for you."

"I mean it, Sarah. I don't even want to think about the dark places my mind could have gone last night after everything with my mom. I've wasted so much time dreading that moment, worrying about what the truth would mean, but your presence made it all okay. You're like a magician."

A magician. A miracle. Both wonderful things to be called, but not quite what she was hoping for. It was hard to blame him. He'd been through so much with his family. It was no wonder that he was closed off, that he'd shored up his defenses so solidly that no woman had managed to make her way inside. She had to appreciate that he'd come so far since she'd met him. Maybe he needed a nudge. Maybe he needed to know that she wouldn't hurt him, that she would give her heart to him just as freely as she'd given her body.

Just do it. Just say it and let it come out. Open your heart. "I love you, Aiden." A warm wave hit her—contentment, satisfaction, accomplishment all rolled into one. This time she'd finally gotten it. She smiled and gazed into his eyes, but it became clear—within a few heartbeats—that something was wrong. His eyes weren't indifferent or angry...they were hurt. It wasn't at all what she'd expected. Of the many things she could've seen, that was not on the list of possible reactions to *I love you.*

Sixteen

I love you? No. This isn't happening.

Aiden had never before wanted so badly to be able to rattle off a string of words, but he couldn't. *I love you* was forever, and he wasn't ready for that. He was ready to ask if he could see her after their ten days were up, but the words she'd just said had ruined that possibility. There was only one good response, and he couldn't go there. "I don't take love lightly." In truth, he didn't take—or give—romantic love at all. He'd never told a woman he loved her. He'd never felt it. His relationship with Sarah was different, but they'd been caught in extraordinary circumstances and his feelings for Oliver were intertwined with his perception of her. Could it be love? His gut wasn't answering.

"I don't take it lightly either," Sarah pleaded. "But I

love you. I know we haven't known each other for long, but this is what's in my heart. I had to say it."

Frustration nipped at him like an angry dog. Why was she pushing this? Why did she have to take such a huge leap? He was racing to keep up, out of control, with no idea where or how this would end. "I have feelings for you, Sarah. And they're good feelings. I'm just not ready to go there yet. It's too soon." Did people fall in love in ten days? If they did, what happened to those people? Were they still in love a year later? What if everything between them faded and fizzled?

"It's not too soon for me. Some people fall in love in a minute. There is no timetable."

"But there is for us. You just spent the last ten days reminding me of a deadline. I don't like the idea of being forced into something." He hated his biting tone, but he saw her as his safe place, and she'd turned that inside out. She was sabotaging what was between them, just as she had in Miami. This time, she wasn't making a unilateral decision. She'd pulled him into this one and forced him to participate. Did she not see that he'd already taken big steps with her? He'd never spent more than three days with a woman.

"Forced? You made the first move last night." She sat up in bed and yanked the covers over her. "And you knew I was leaving tomorrow, but you took me to bed anyway, knowing that you didn't have an inkling of serious feelings for me?"

"Of course I knew you were leaving. You've spent every waking minute of our time together reminding me of it."

"And that made it easy to sleep with me. No pesky Sarah to worry about after tomorrow."

"That's not fair. I wanted you. I still want you." At least he could say that much without reservation.

Oliver yelped over the baby monitor. Aiden tossed back the comforter and pulled on his boxer shorts. "I'll get him. We'll have to finish talking about this later. I don't want to argue in front of the baby."

Sarah rolled away from him. "Honestly? I don't want to talk about it at all."

"Why not?"

"Because there's no coming back from what I just said to you."

She wasn't wrong about that.

Aiden stalked down the hall, his mind reeling. He'd been thinking he might invite Sarah to spend next weekend with them, and see how that went. He certainly hadn't been thinking about labels. Love hadn't crossed his mind. It wasn't even on the map.

He opened the door to Oliver's room. The little guy was standing, holding on to the top rail of his crib, unsteady on the mattress. He bounced up and down when he saw Aiden, squealing and grinning. He picked up Oliver and kissed him on the forehead, holding him close. Two labels he didn't have to question were that of father and son. What they shared was love. But he wasn't able to put a label on what he felt for Sarah. And if he told her what she wanted to hear, just to make her happy for now, and it later ended up hurting her, he'd never forgive himself. He might not be able to say *I love you, too*, but that was better than taking it back later.

He changed Oliver and brought him down to the kitchen, warming up a bottle and sitting with him on the sofa in the living room. He tried to read the rhythm of Sarah's footsteps upstairs—there was no telling what she was doing, but she was busy. Was she pacing the floor, angry with him because he'd let her down? Was she re-thinking what she'd said? Was she doing the inevitable—packing up to leave? He wouldn't blame her if she were, no matter how much it might hurt. She was a vibrant and beautiful young woman. Any man in the world would be a fool to say no to her, making Aiden a class A idiot. Still, he couldn't lie to her. He couldn't say he loved her when he wasn't sure what it meant.

His loose plan of asking if she wanted to date, al-though tantamount to picking out china for him, would clearly not be enough for her. Not now.

I love you.

Yeah, I'm not sure. Can we just go out to dinner?

Starting on dramatically different pages wasn't a rec-ipe for romantic success. It was a setup for disaster. She'd already been hurt by the guy she worked for. He wouldn't hurt her like that—he was different. So maybe he was back to where he'd thought he'd needed to be a few days ago—preserve the friendship and set aside romance.

Sarah was about to wear a rut in the hardwood floor of Aiden's guest room. *How could I have been so stupid?*

When it came right down to it, Aiden was a case of unrequited love. And although it stung like crazy, at least Sarah knew what it was. The heartache ahead had a name. A *label*. She could say with confidence,

I left because it was unrequited love. He wouldn't say it back to me and I'd already said it to him, so I had to leave. How does a girl come back from that? Her friends would answer, *You don't come back from that. You leave. With your head held high and your dignity in place.* And Sarah could smile and nod, knowing she'd done the right thing. Even when the moments came when she was crumbling to dust on the inside, she would know she'd had no choice.

Oliver was another matter. She'd already been destroyed by the notion of leaving him, precisely her fear. His place in her heart would always be there. Their relationship was quite the opposite of unrequited. It was the purest love she'd ever known. Aside from her family's, Oliver's love was the only love she'd never doubted. She saw it on Oliver's face when she walked into his room in the morning or when he'd woken up from a nap. She felt it when he was upset and she held him close, the two of them clinging to each other. She lived and breathed their love when he laughed. Oliver's love had filled her heart for a month and its absence would leave an unimaginable void, and there wasn't anything to do about it. Oliver belonged with his father, and his father didn't love her.

She slumped down on the bench at the foot of the bed. "Now what?" she asked aloud. She couldn't go downstairs and talk about this more. It would only hurt. And she wasn't going to try to convince Aiden that he loved her. She wanted him to just love her. She didn't much like the idea of hiding out in her room until tomorrow. That left only one option, the one Aiden had

so generously provided her with yesterday after decid-
ing on the nanny—leave today.

She wasn't ready to say goodbye to Oliver, but the
truth was that she'd never be ready. She could spend a
lifetime preparing and it would never make it any easier.

Her phone beeped with a notification. She walked
over to the bedside table and looked at the screen—it
was an email, from Katie.

Sarah,
Despite the gaps in your financial forecast, Sylvia would
still like to continue talks about acquiring Kama. Sylvia
and I would like to come to Boston first thing Monday
morning to tour your facility, look over designs for next
year and discuss our options. Does 9 a.m. suit you? I
know today's Saturday, but I need to know ASAP.
Best,
Katie

How many signs could Sarah get from the universe
before she stopped fighting? Aiden hadn't returned *I
love you.* Sylvia Hodge wanted her back in Boston,
ready to talk business. And she'd set Oliver up for the
life she wanted him to have. That meant Sarah needed
to say goodbye, get on the next train and not look back.

She typed her reply.

Katie,
Thanks so much. Tell Sylvia I will see you both Monday
morning. Looking forward to it.
Sarah

With no more time wasted on overthinking, she got out her suitcase and started packing. The sooner she got out, the better. Luckily, she didn't have much, so it only took a few minutes. She then hopped in the shower, cleaned up and dressed in the same old sundress she'd worn the day she met Aiden. That seemed like a lifetime ago.

As she took each step down the stairs, the tears threatened to take over. She imagined it was like trying to get out of the ocean when a storm has come up out of nowhere. The waves roll you back as you swim, the tide pulling just as hard, ocean spray in your face, but you keep going because you have to get to shore. You have to save yourself. For what, you aren't sure. You only know that it's your instinct to survive. You'll do anything to make it.

She and her suitcase reached the landing. She raised the handle, and rolled it toward the foyer.

Aiden's voice from the kitchen stopped her dead in her tracks. "You're leaving?"

Oliver was playing on the floor with some plastic bowls and wooden spoons.

She bit into her lower lip. *You can do this.* "Yes. I have to. I got an email from Sylvia Hodge's office. They need me in Boston ready to talk Monday morning. I need time to prepare. And you don't need me anymore, so I might as well get out of your hair and let you and Oliver enjoy your weekend."

"Sarah. We didn't even finish talking about everything." He came out from behind the kitchen island, but thankfully didn't touch her. He instead crossed his arms. "We're just going to leave it all unsaid?"

She forced a smile and an enthusiastic nod. She'd never felt less happy or eager to do anything. "I don't think we need to talk about it anymore. I get it, Aiden. I do. I'm not going to try to get you to say things that aren't in your heart. You didn't do anything wrong."

"I just wish you'd give me some time to wrap my head around it."

The thing was—she didn't need more time. She knew exactly how much she loved him. She felt it in the depths of her belly right now, a terrible burning. She knew exactly how bad it was going to hurt to step onto that elevator. She couldn't wait. She couldn't give him another chance. Aiden might never get to the place she needed him to get to. It wasn't his fault. He'd been deeply hurt by his past. And he'd always been very upfront—he needed space.

"It's okay. I shouldn't have said anything this morning. Just forget it." She rushed over to Oliver and crouched down, raising his face with the tip of her finger. "Goodbye, sweet…" her voice cracked into a million pieces. Her lip shook. Her chest convulsed. She couldn't say it. Her heart wouldn't let her. She leaned down and placed a single kiss on the top of his head, committing to memory his smell and the feel of his soft curls against her lips. She would miss that so much. Forever.

She straightened and turned away from Aiden. The tears were streaming down her face in a deluge and she couldn't let him know that he'd gotten to her like this. "I have to go. I'll miss my train."

"Are you sure about this?" he asked, doing the thing she'd dreaded—grasping her arm.

She didn't look back. She hid. "I'm sure."

"At least let me call down to John and have him take you to the station. Let me do that much. Just to say thank you for everything."

Don't fight him. Just go. Just walk out. Save yourself. She nodded. "Okay. Great. Thanks."

With that, she rushed to the elevator, jabbed the button and walked on board. She dropped her head as the door closed, her tears dotting the floor. She couldn't look up. She couldn't watch everything she'd ever wanted disappear.

Sarah went immediately into autopilot, putting on her sunglasses to hide her eyes and marching through the lobby outside. Luckily, John was always waiting for Aiden—this time it paid off for her.

"Ms. Daltrey. Penn Station?"

"Yes. John. Thanks." She climbed into the backseat, sucking in a trembling breath. *Just get me to the train. Then I'll be okay.*

Her phone beeped with a text from Aiden.

This is stupid. Come back. We should talk.

Words weren't enough this morning. Not sure what's different now.

I need time. I'm sorry.

It's okay.

She stopped herself from typing the words she wanted to. *I still love you even though you don't love me.*

"Ms. Daltrey?" John asked from the front seat. "I have a message from Mr. Langford. He's asking me to bring you back to the house."

She blew out a breath. It was just like Aiden to snap his fingers and expect the world to conform to his wishes. "No. Please don't do that. Just pull over and drop me off and I'll get in a cab."

"Ma'am? I don't want to leave you, either."

Every sad feeling she'd had a few minutes ago was turning to frustration. "I'll text Mr. Langford. Please just keep driving."

She tapped out a message to Aiden.

Please don't put John in the middle of this. Let me go.

Waiting for Aiden's response was agony. She didn't want to argue. But she wasn't ready for the end, again.

Ok.

She tucked her phone into her bag. "All straightened out, John. It was just a misunderstanding."

"Oh, good. Okay. I'll have you at the station in no time."

"Great. The sooner, the better."

Seventeen

Day ten arrived with sunshine streaming through the windows and a giddy Oliver, full of energy and ready to take on the day. Right after breakfast, they'd started doing laps in the house. From the kitchen to the library to his office and back, Oliver walked while Daddy followed, holding his little hands to steady him. Oliver had discovered this new routine while they'd been playing last night before bed. Judging by the way he took to it and the enthusiasm with which he cruised along furniture, he'd be walking and running in a matter of days.

Aiden, however happy he was to share this milestone with Oliver, was dragging—no sleep and a gaping hole in your heart will do that to a guy.

Sarah was gone. And her absence was much more noticeable than Aiden had expected. The house felt strange and incomplete. Had it felt like this before she came along? He couldn't recall, exactly. It was quite different with Oliver there, but still, it wasn't the same without Sarah.

He missed everything about her—the way she hummed when she puttered around in the kitchen and her sweet smell when she walked past him. The way her face lit up when she laughed and the way she wouldn't let him get away with anything when she was mad. Memories shuffled through his mind—the day she managed to talk her way into one of the most secure office buildings in the world. She'd made his entire life turn on a dime that day, and done it in unflappable fashion. That night in the bathtub, when he'd first bonded with Oliver and Sarah had made it happen. That was also the night he'd caught her staring at him, the night he'd foolishly thought that seducing her would be like taking any other woman to bed. He'd relied on their ten-day deadline then. It made it easier for him to get what he wanted, no strings attached. Little did he know that Sarah was capable of tying up his heart and his head with those strings…and tugging them all the way back to Boston.

But what was he supposed to do? They were operating at different speeds. She was comfortable with bold strides. He needed to ease into it. He knew no other way.

His phone rang from the kitchen counter. His pulse picked up. Was it Sarah? He steered Oliver over and consulted the screen. Anna. Not the call he wanted, but maybe she could tell him to stop being such a wimp.

"Hey," Aiden said. "This is a surprise. It's a little early isn't it?"

"I figured you were already up with Oliver and I wanted to check in on you after the other night with Mom. How are you holding up?"

Aiden dragged a barstool around the kitchen island so he had a good view of Oliver, and sat down. "I'm doing fine. I've had years to stew over it. It's more of a relief than anything. And at least we can all get together now without it being hopelessly uncomfortable."

Anna blew out a breath. "Good. I'm glad you feel that way because I have something else I need to talk to you about. Jacob told me I should probably just butt out, and we kind of had a big argument about it, but I don't want to butt out. I can't not say something."

"What in the world are you talking about?"

"Sarah, Aiden. Don't you dare let her go back to Boston today without you two making a plan to keep seeing each other. I know how you are and I'm telling you right now that she's not like other women. She's a keeper, Aiden. I don't want you to blow it just because you've convinced yourself it's easier to play the field."

Aiden could only imagine what his face looked like right now—pure shock. Astonishment. "First off, why don't you tell me how you really feel? And second, how do you know there was anything going on between us?"

Anna huffed at what she apparently saw as Aiden's absurdity. "I saw the way you two were looking at each other the other night. And the minute that all of that stuff went down with Mom, she was the one you turned to. Right away. You didn't even hesitate. It's so obvious to me that you two are in love."

"How can you tell that from a look?"

"Am I wrong? There are feelings between you two, aren't there?"

"Well, yes, there are feelings between us. But that doesn't mean it's love. And besides, it's too late. She's already gone."

"What?" Anna shouted so loudly, she nearly blew out Aiden's eardrum.

"Careful or you'll go into labor."

"You let her leave? Why did you do that? Why would you be so stupid?"

Because she said she loved me and I couldn't say it back. The realization hit him, and the repercussions came at him just as hard. "It was moving too fast for me."

"The man who jumps out of airplanes thought it was moving too fast? Sounds to me like you're confused."

"Yeah. I guess I am. I just don't want to make a mistake. She means a lot to me. But I can't tell her I love her if I'm not sure. I don't even know how I'm supposed to know if it's really love. People always say that you'll know when it happens. Well, I don't know."

"Let me ask you this. How do you feel now that she's gone?"

"Horrible. Like somebody ripped my heart out of my chest."

"And what's the house like without her there?"

"Terrible. I'm thinking Oliver and I might need to move."

"And if you could do anything at all right now, what would you do?"

"Go see her. Apologize." *Oh God. I love her.* Aiden cast his sights down at Oliver, who was hitting the floor with a wooden spoon. *I really am an idiot. I'm a complete jerk.* He'd said to himself many times over the past ten days that he would never let Oliver go without. But in letting Sarah leave, he was not only depriving Oliver of the perfect mother, he was keeping himself from the one person who understood him and loved him despite his faults. Oliver had shown him unconditional love. But so had Sarah.

"Do you enjoy feeling like this?" Anna asked. "Because you know you can fix it."

"I can't fix it. I ruined it. She told me she loved me and I didn't say it back."

Anna gasped on the other end of the line.

"That's pretty much the end, isn't it?" His conscience was impossibly heavy. He'd trampled all over the heart of the woman he loved. "I mean, how do I come back from that?"

"Groveling."

"Groveling?"

"It's the only thing that works. Flowers help. Jewelry. Chocolate. A gift certificate for a massage. But mostly groveling. You need to get your butt up to Boston and beg for her forgiveness. You need to tell her how you feel."

"You think it will work?"

"Not sure, but I think you'll regret it forever if you

don't try. Jacob and I can be over in a half hour to watch the baby."

None of this will be right without Oliver. "No. It's okay. I'm taking him with me."

Sarah went into the Kama office Sunday morning. Although it was their headquarters, that word was generous—it was really just an old warehouse she'd been renting for the last year. Sleep last night had been pointless—too many painful things wreaking havoc in her head. Too many things running through her heart, like water through a sieve. She'd been so scared of what would happen if she got too close and now she knew how right she'd been to fear it. Losing Oliver and Aiden was the worst thing that had ever happened to her. No doubt about that.

She didn't bother flipping on the lights as she wound through the sewing room with its massive cutting tables, stacked high with boxes of inventory ready to ship. She went straight back to her office and got to work— the act of a woman invested in her own success, but it felt like an empty gesture. A show. More faking it. Her heart wasn't in it, as much as she might very well be standing on the precipice of great success. On the inside, she was as empty as she'd ever been, which was a devastating realization. Her hard work was finally paying off, and she felt horrible. She'd seen low moments, but not like this.

Not like last night, when she couldn't get a single minute of relief because her eyes were like a faucet. Her heart had stubbornly chosen to ache and throb in her chest and remind her with every pointless beat that the difference between the love a person gives freely and the love they receive in return is what ends up breaking us. This was the second time she'd had to learn the lesson of how it empties a person—giving and giving, never refilling the tank. And she was as done as done could be. The fate of her business felt as inconsequential as a speck of dust floating in air. It was nothing worth holding on to if she couldn't have what she'd truly invested in—Aiden and Oliver.

But Aiden hadn't been able to go there. He just couldn't say *I love you*. If only he knew—or cared—three little words and she would've figured out a way to stay. She would've told him that she'd meant it. She would've done everything she could to make them all whole again, to knit them into the family they could have been. But apparently, for a man wealthy beyond anything she ever imagined, three words was too high a price to pay.

She tidied her office—going through the mail she'd missed over the last week, filing away things, neatening stacks of paper. She made sure her computer screen was free of smudges, and watered the pink orchid on her desk. She did every mindless task she could come up with, all in the interest of staying busy. If she couldn't move forward, she could at least tread water. She could keep her head above the rising tide. She had to fight back her thoughts of her last night with Aiden, of the connection they'd shared. There was no doubt in her mind that it had been more than sex that night. And she knew, deep down, that Aiden knew it, too. He just couldn't admit it to himself. He was too wounded.

Tessa popped into view. "Morning," she said, stepping foot into the office.

Sarah jumped. "You scared me." She pressed her hand to her chest. Her heart was pounding. "What are you doing here? You didn't need to come in today. You should be at home relaxing. Tomorrow's a big day. I need you on top of your game."

A mischievous smile spread across her face. "I came by to let somebody in. He was pretty sure you weren't going to let him in on your own."

"What? Who?"

Just then, Aiden appeared in her doorway, Oliver in his arms. "I had to talk my way in. I needed to bring Oliver to you. He misses you. I miss you."

The grin on Tessa's face had only grown. "I'll leave you three alone. See you tomorrow."

Sarah walked out from behind her desk, in shock. Was this a dream? Were Aiden and Oliver a mirage? Surely a figment of her imagination couldn't have the pull on her that Aiden did right now. All she wanted to do was fling her arms around him and kiss him. Oliver reached for her. The minute she had him, Aiden's arms were around them both.

"Sarah, I'm here because I had to tell you in person that I love you."

"But…" Tears rolled down her face. How could she possibly cry more? "You don't have to do this. Don't feel like you have to say that to me. And you really shouldn't feel like you have to travel hours with a baby to say that to me in person."

"But I do have to do those things. I have to make it up to you. And I have to tell you the truth." He loosened his grip, to see her better. "I've been falling in love with you since the first night, when you put me in the bathtub with this little guy. It's grown so fast that I didn't know what it was. I couldn't see it. I don't know if I was afraid or confused or what, but the minute you left, I knew it wasn't right."

She nodded eagerly, feeling as though a weight had been lifted. Her hunch had been right. And it hadn't taken long for Aiden to see it, too. "I know it happened fast. I thought I was crazy to say that to you yesterday, but I had to. Especially after everything with your family." She studied his face, his blue eyes nearly taking her breath away. "I couldn't not tell you that I love you. You deserved to know."

He sighed and looped her hair behind her ear, caressing her cheek. "I've spent my whole life homesick for a home I never even knew. And you showed up out of nowhere, and made that home for me in ten days."

"Technically, it was nine."

A breathy laugh left his lips. "You showed me what love is. You opened up my closed-up heart. And that heart is going to shrivel up and die without you. The home you built isn't going to work without you."

"What are you saying, Aiden?"

"I'm saying that I love you and we have to find a way to make this work."

"But you're in New York. I'm here. How are we

going to manage that? You don't even have a permanent nanny."

"I called Lily from the plane and convinced her to
take the job. She's flying up here tomorrow morning to
take care of Oliver while I go into the LangTel regional
office downtown for a few hours."

Sarah wasn't sure she was hearing him correctly.
"You're going to hang out in Boston? For how long?"

He shrugged. "Depends on what Sylvia Hodge tells
you tomorrow. Then we'll figure it out. Anna said that if
Sylvia acquires Kama, she'll probably ask you to work
out of New York so you're available for meetings and
are more plugged in to the industry."

Sarah hadn't considered that. It was all still so new.
"So we wait and see what happens tomorrow?"

"I was hoping Oliver and I can move in with you for
a few days. I figure we'll put Lily in a hotel."

"I don't know. I need my space."

Aiden laughed and kissed the top of her head. "Darling, as long as you come back to me, you can have all
the space you need."

Eighteen

For the third weekend in a row, Sarah was back in New York with Aiden and Oliver. She looked forward to these days more than anything, even when the back and forth was tiresome. Only one more week and the Kama office would move to Sylvia Hodge's Manhattan headquarters. She'd be in the city full-time. She, Aiden and Oliver would be together. Even though she and Aiden hadn't discussed their future, Sarah was more than content. It hadn't seemed necessary and her forcing of *I love you* had flopped—at least at first. Plus, Aiden was a complicated guy. Commitment wasn't easy for him. Just knowing that he loved her and wanted to be with her was enough for now.

Everything else workwise was already in place— when Sylvia decided to acquire Kama, it came together very fast. Last week, they'd moved everything into a new manufacturing space outside Boston. It was ten times bigger than the original facility and the air-conditioning worked—no small matter now that it was the middle of June. They'd hired ten new assembly people, three more employees to manage the warehouse. Tessa was overseeing the production facility, and she'd received a big fat raise for taking on her new responsibilities. Sarah couldn't have been any happier about being able to reward her for a job well done. The change also left much more time for Sarah to spend on designing, selecting fabrics and planning out the next several seasons. It was hard to believe, but everything on the work front was really coming together.

Saturdays at Aiden's were pretty low-key. Today had been no different, although they were anxiously awaiting a call from Jacob since Anna had gone into labor that morning. To pass the time, Sarah and Aiden had taken Oliver for a long walk, then grabbed some lunch. The baby had his nap after that, and they turned their dinner into a picnic up on the rooftop terrace. Now that it was nearly eight, Sarah was getting a bit of work done in Aiden's home office. Oliver was already in bed and Aiden had camped out with a book in the library.

Aiden's phone, which he'd left on the desk, rang. She glanced at the screen and grabbed it. "Oh my God. Aiden!" she yelled out. "It's Jacob. Get in here!" She answered the call. "Jacob? Aiden's in the other room. I figured I should answer. Is there news?"

"It's a girl," he said triumphantly. "Eight pounds,

seven ounces. Twenty-one inches long. Big head of thick, black hair. She's beautiful."

Sarah loved hearing the good news, but Aiden was missing it. She got up from the desk to search for him. "Congratulations. I'm so happy. How's Anna?" She reached the library. No Aiden. *Weird.*

"She's tired, but she's doing great. We're both relieved the baby's finally here and she's healthy. It's been such a rocky road."

"Oh, I know. She's your miracle baby. It's wonderful." Into the kitchen she traveled. Still no Aiden. "Do you have a name yet?"

"Grace. It's Anna's middle name."

Sarah glanced into the living room, which was also empty. "That's so beautiful. You must be so thrilled."

"I am, but I also have a million more phone calls to make. If you could tell Aiden, that'd be great. I'm sure Anna will want to speak to you both at some point."

Up the stairs Sarah went. "I don't know if you guys will be up for it, but we have Oliver's birthday party next Saturday."

"Oh, right. We'll have to see how it goes, I guess. We might need to call you for some baby advice."

"Absolutely no problem. Whatever you need. Love to all three of you. Can't wait to see her." She ended the call, but didn't dare yell now that she was in the hall. She'd wake Oliver. Where in the world was Aiden?

The door to his bedroom was closed. Now that they'd been cohabitating for nearly a month, she didn't hesitate to open it. But the knob wouldn't turn. It was locked.

She leaned against the door, but heard nothing. She

rapped quietly and waited. She couldn't text him—she had his phone. She knocked again. Finally, he answered.

"Hey," he said, seeming flustered. He raked his hand through his hair, poking his head through the narrow opening he'd left.

"Your sister had a baby girl. Her name is Grace. That's what's up. Where have you been?"

His shoulders dropped. "Damn. I can't believe I missed that call. That's a bummer. Is everything okay?"

"Everything's great. I told them you send your best." She tried to peek into his room, but could see nothing. "What are you doing in there? Can I come in?" He was behaving so strangely.

"I'm working on something. A surprise. But it's not ready."

She laughed quietly, curious what he was up to. Her birthday wasn't until October. "Like that's not cryptic. Do you want me to go away?"

"No. No. It's okay. I was going to call you up in a minute anyway. Just close your eyes and I'll lead you to the bed."

"If that's where we're going, it's not a surprise. Not that I won't enjoy it immensely." She elbowed him in the stomach, but he didn't take the joke. He was dead serious, so she decided to follow orders.

"Just a minute," he said when she was seated on the bed. "Be right back."

With her eyes closed, she listened for clues. He started singing. She'd never heard Aiden sing. Not once.

"How's it going in there?" she asked.

"You're so impatient." His voice was close—as if he

were right next to her. He took her hand and she opened her eyes. "Ready?" He had a huge grin on his face.

"Yes." She trailed behind him into the bathroom. The lights were off. The marble countertops were covered in an array of lit candles. "Ooh. Bath night. So romantic."

"I had to make it romantic. For you."

She wrapped her arms around his waist, and he planted a soft and sensuous kiss on her lips. "That's adorable. I love that you made an extra effort for our Saturday night together."

He kissed her again, on her cheek, beneath her ear, on that extrasensitive spot on her neck. "It's more special than that."

Again, with the clues and mysterious phrasings. His kisses, however amazing, weren't helping. They made it difficult to think straight. "What kind of special?"

He cupped the side of her face and caressed her cheek with his thumb. "You're the best thing that's ever happened to me. I don't want to let you go."

Let me go? Oh my God. She clapped her hand over her mouth. "Aiden. Are you?"

"Shh. Just let me ask." He plucked a washcloth from the counter. A blue Tiffany box was beneath it. He popped it open, smiling wide and presenting her with the most gorgeous diamond ring she'd ever seen. "I love you so much. I want you to be my wife and Oliver's mother. Will you marry me?"

She blinked away tears, her heart about to burst from pure joy. "Yes. Of course." He placed the ring on her finger, and she popped up onto her toes, kissing him hard before stealing the chance to admire the diamond.

"It's so gorgeous. Did you tell the people at Tiffany you were going to ask me in the bathroom?"

He laughed. "No. Do you know why I chose this room?"

She shrugged. "Because you like taking a shower with me?"

"That's part of it, but not the real reason." He took her left hand, straightening the ring. "That first night we gave Oliver a bath was the beginning of our life together. As a family. I wanted to acknowledge the start before we step into our future."

Tears welled again. "That is the sweetest thing ever."

"That was also the first time I caught you staring at me. That was sort of a big deal."

She swatted his arm. "I can't help it. You're just way too hot." Whatever she'd done to be lucky enough to have Aiden, she was glad she'd done it.

He cranked the faucet on the tub and turned his attention to her top, lifting it over her head. His heavenly lips skimmed her shoulder. "I can't wait to get in this bathtub with you and make love to you all night and talk about our future together."

Their future together. "Now I don't have to worry about the perfect guy walking into my life. I found him."

"Actually, I'm pretty sure you walked into his."

* * * * *

COMING NEXT MONTH FROM

Available May 9, 2017

#2515 THE MARRIAGE CONTRACT
Billionaires and Babies • by Kat Cantrell
Longing for a child of his own, reclusive billionaire Des marries McKenna in name only so she can bear his child, but when complications force them to live as man and wife, the temptation is to make the marriage real...

#2516 TRIPLETS FOR THE TEXAN
Texas Cattleman's Club: Blackmail • by Janice Maynard
Wealthy Texas doctor Troy "Hutch" Hutchinson is the one who got away. Now he's back and ready to make things right, but Simone is already expecting three little surprises of her own...

#2517 LITTLE SECRET, RED HOT SCANDAL
Las Vegas Nights • by Cat Schield
Superstar Nate Tucker has no interest in the spoiled pop princess determined to ensnare him, but when a secret affair with her quiet sister, Mia, results in a baby on the way, he'll do whatever it takes to claim Mia as his.

#2518 THE RANCHER'S CINDERELLA BRIDE
Callahan's Clan • by Sara Orwig
When Gabe agrees to a fake engagement with his best friend, Meg, he doesn't expect to fight temptation at every turn. But a makeover leads to the wildest kiss of his life and now he wants to find out if friends make the best lovers...

#2519 THE MAGNATE'S MARRIAGE MERGER
The McNeill Magnates • by Joanne Rock
Matchmaker Lydia Whitney has been secretly exacting revenge on her wealthy ex-lover, but when he discovers her true identity, it's his turn to exact the sweetest revenge...by making her his convenient wife!

#2520 TYCOON COWBOY'S BABY SURPRISE
The Wild Caruthers Bachelors • by Katherine Garbera
What happens in Vegas should stay there, but when Kinley Quinten shows up in Cole's Hill, Texas, to plan a wedding, the groom's very familiar brother's attempts to rekindle their fling is hindered by a little secret she kept years ago...

HDCNM0417

SPECIAL EXCERPT FROM

HARLEQUIN™ *Desire*

*Superstar Nate Tucker has no interest in the spoiled pop
princess determined to ensnare him, but when a secret
affair with her quiet sister, Mia, results in a baby on the
way, he'll do whatever it takes to claim Mia as his.*

Read on for a sneak peek at
LITTLE SECRET, RED HOT SCANDAL
by Cat Schield

Mia had made her choice and it hadn't been him.

"How've you been?" He searched her face for some
sign she'd suffered as he had, lingering over the circles
under her eyes and the downward turn to her mouth. To
his relief she didn't look happy, but that didn't stop her
from putting on a show.

"Things have been great."

"Tell me the truth." He was asking after her welfare,
but what he really wanted to know was if she'd missed
him.

"I'm great. Really."

"I hope your sister gave you a little time off."

"Ivy was invited to a charity event in South Beach and
we extended our stay a couple days to kick back and soak
up some sun."

Ivy demanded all Mia's time and energy. That Nate
had spent any alone time with Mia during Ivy's eight-
week stint on his tour was nothing short of amazing.

They'd snuck around like teenage kids. The danger of getting caught promoted intimacy. And at first, Nate found the subterfuge amusing. It got old fast.

It had bothered Nate that Ivy treated Mia like an employee instead of a sister. She never seemed to appreciate how Mia's kind and thoughtful behavior went above and beyond the role of personal assistant.

"I don't like the way we left things between us," Nate declared, taking a step in her direction.

Mia took a matching step backward. "You asked for something I couldn't give you."

"I asked for you to come to Las Vegas with me."

"We'd barely known each other two months." It was the same excuse she'd given him three weeks ago and it rang as hollow now as it had then. "And I couldn't leave Ivy."

"She could've found another assistant." He'd said the same thing the morning after the tour ended. The night after Mia had stayed with him until the sun crested the horizon.

"I'm not just her assistant. I'm her sister," Mia said, now as then. "She needs me."

I need you.

He wouldn't repeat the words. It wouldn't do any good. She'd still choose obligation to her sister over being happy with him.

And he couldn't figure out why.

HARLEQUIN® *Desire*

AVAILABLE MAY 2017

TRIPLETS FOR THE TEXAN

BY *USA TODAY* BESTSELLING AUTHOR

JANICE MAYNARD,

PART OF THE SIZZLING
TEXAS CATTLEMAN'S CLUB: BLACKMAIL SERIES.

Wealthy Texas doctor Troy "Hutch" Hutchinson is the one who got away. Now he's back and ready to make things right, but Simone is already expecting three little surprises of her own...

AND DON'T MISS A SINGLE INSTALLMENT OF

TEXAS CATTLEMAN'S CLUB:

BLACKMAIL

No secret—or heart—is safe in Royal, Texas...

The Tycoon's Secret Child
by *USA TODAY* bestselling author Maureen Child

Two-Week Texas Seduction by Cat Schield

Reunited with the Rancher
by *USA TODAY* bestselling author Sara Orwig

Expecting the Billionaire's Baby by Andrea Laurence

Triplets for the Texan
by *USA TODAY* bestselling author Janice Maynard

AND

Whatever You're Into… Passionate Reads

Looking for more passionate reads from Harlequin®?
Fear not! Harlequin® Presents, Harlequin® Desire and
Harlequin® Blaze offer you irresistible romance stories
featuring powerful heroes.

◈HARLEQUIN *Presents.*

Do you want alpha males, decadent glamour and jet-set
lifestyles? Step into the sensational, sophisticated world of
Harlequin® Presents, where sinfully tempting heroes ignite a
fierce and wickedly irresistible passion!

◈HARLEQUIN *Desire*

Harlequin® Desire novels are powerful, passionate and
provocative contemporary romances set against a backdrop of
wealth, privilege and sweeping family saga. Alpha heroes with
a soft side meet strong-willed but vulnerable heroines amid a
dramatic world of divided loyalties, high-stakes conflict and
intense emotion.

◈HARLEQUIN *Blaze*

Harlequin® Blaze stories sizzle with strong heroines and
irresistible heroes playing the game of modern love and lust.
They're fun, sexy and always steamy.

Be sure to check out our full selection of books
within each series every month!